Detritus

Detritus

Edited
by

Kate Jonez
S.S. Michaels

Omnium Gatherum
Los Angeles CA

Detritus
Edited by Kate Jonez
and S.S. Michaels
Anthology Copyright © 2011
Individual stories copyright by individual authors
Cover Illustration Copyright © 2011 Kate Jonez

ISBN-13:978-0615587684
ISBN-10:0615587682

First Edition

Stories

Every passion borders on the chaotic, but the collector's passion borders on the chaos of memories.

— Walter Benjamin

Chewed Up

by
Jeremy C. Shipp

Tonight, my wife's hair smells like strawberries. I want to wrap my arm around her, but she would only squirm away, so I don't try.

Instead, I lie there, inches from her, and a world away.

I think about how we used to stay up all night dissecting French films and trying to figure out God, and my chest tightens. My stomach spins. And I feel little balls of anxiety moving up and down my arms.

I say, "I love you, Aubrey."

She's asleep, or pretending to be.

In lonely moments like this, I can't help but think about chewed up bubble gum. I close my eyes, and I see the wads stuck underneath tables and desks and chairs, like little alien pods ready to hatch. I do what I can to clean up the parks and bus stops and train stations, but there's still a whole world of gum out there. Sometimes I fantasize about breaking into my neighbors' houses and purifying the rooms, because you know there's gum in all the nooks and crannies. The neighborhood is full of kids, and kids will put gum anywhere.

Once, when I was young, I snuck into my sister's room, and I smashed a wad of Bazooka Joe in her hair. I don't think there was a reason why. In the morning, my sister screamed at me, my parents screamed at me, but I never admitted my guilt. Even when my sister was in the hospital, I didn't apologize for the gum. I just told her the story about how her cat Zipper lost his tooth, and then she was gone.

"I can't sleep," I whisper. "I'm going downstairs."

Crickets.

In the living room, I sit on Aubrey's side of the couch.

I caress the brown leather arm.

Before I get the chance to turn on the TV, I detect movement out of the corner of my eye. I turn my head, and I watch as one of Aubrey's porcelain unicorns falls off the mantelpiece. My whole body tenses, because I'm sure the unicorn's going to break, and Aubrey will blame me, the way she blames me for everything lately.

But the unicorn flaps its wings and touches down on the coffee table.

I weep, and I'm not sure if it's because I'm frightened by the fact that I've gone insane, or just relieved.

The unicorn sits on the obituary section of the newspaper and says, "Why do I always get the crybabies?" She sounds a little like my wife, only higher pitched. What Aubrey would sound like if she were a cartoon character.

I rub my forehead with both hands.

"If you're trying to massage away the madness, that's not gonna work. I'm not going anywhere until your life is a little less fucked up."

"You're never leaving then," I say.

"Stop being so dramatic. It's true that you're a fuck-up of epic proportions and no one can help you. But lucky for you, I'm just the no one for the job."

The unicorn flies over and lands on my lap. She walks around in a circle, then plops over, just like Zipper used to.

"We'll start tomorrow," she says. "Do you want to watch Conan?"

"Alright."

I pet the unicorn. She purrs.

The purity of this creature rubs off on me a little, perhaps magically, and I dream of me and my sister racing to the old scarecrow and back. I don't win. I don't care. Eventually, the magic wears off, and I'm dreaming of hospitals.

Next morning, I go the park and get to work purifying one of the picnic tables. I use my putty knife to scrape off wad after wad.

The unicorn paces back and forth under the table. "Any idea why Aubrey's giving you the cold shoulder?"

"No," I say, and I drop a red wad into the Ziploc bag.

"Can you find out?"

"She won't talk to me."

The unicorn stops pacing and looks up at me. "Does she have a diary?"

"That's not going to happen."

Hours later, I'm in the bedroom, searching through Aubrey's drawers. Aubrey's home, but there's no chance she'll walk in on me. When I'm upstairs, she's downstairs, and vice versa.

Finally, I find the diary, which turns out to be a dream journal. No wonder she always writes in the morning right after she wakes up.

I read through the last few entries.

"So?" the unicorn says, poking my arm with her hoof.

"She dreams a lot about a baby boy. He drowns in a bathtub and falls off a skyscraper and gets pulled apart by dogs. Aubrey always tries to save him, but she can't."

"Well, you're a pathetic crybaby, so the baby obviously represents you."

"Funny."

"I'm not kidding. My guess is that Aubrey needs you to grow up and be a man."

"I work hard. I respect her. What more does she want from me?"

Minutes later, I'm watching ESPN in the living room, and I hear Aubrey moving around upstairs.

The unicorn stomps on the remote control and turns up the volume. "If she can't hear you, then what's the point?"

After the game's over, I say, "I'm off to the gym!"

Me and the unicorn get in the Prius. "Do you think I

should get a Hummer or a truck or something?"

"Couldn't hurt."

"Do you really think this is what she wants?"

The unicorn shrugs, as well as a unicorn can shrug.

I start the car.

Weeks later, and we're back in the park, purifying a wrought iron bench.

"Any progress?" the porcelain beast says.

"She still won't talk to me," I say.

"Shit."

"Any other bright ideas?"

"Just one. But it's a bit fucked up."

She tells me her plan, and she's right. It is fucked up.

"You in?" the unicorn says, and holds out her hoof.

I touch the hoof with my finger. "Fine."

On the way out of the park, we pass by a garbage can.

The flying horse points a hoof at my Ziploc bag full of gum. "Aren't you going to throw that away?"

"I need them for my collection," I say.

"You're shitting me. Right?"

I shake my head. I can't remember when I started my collection, and to be honest, I don't know where in the house I keep all the gum. But it's as important to me as the unicorns are to Aubrey.

Later, I'm lying beside Aubrey, inches from her, and a world away. Tonight, her hair smells like cherries.

Before I can fall asleep, I detect movement out of the corner of my eye. I turn my head, and I watch as a dark mass flies around the room.

"You're dead, Aubrey!" the creature says. "Dead!"

My wife screams.

The creature flies straight at her face, but I grab the monster just in time and I toss it out the window. The unicorn winks at me before flying off into the night.

After I secure the lock, Aubrey hugs me from behind.

"Thank you," she says, and she leads me to the bed. She smiles at me the way she used to. She pulls off her Pink Floyd t-shirt.

4

So Aubrey doesn't want a man, after all. She wants a hero.

I kiss my wife's forehead, her neck, her stomach, and every kiss tastes different. Cherry, cinnamon, spearmint.

The unicorn crashes through the window and says, "You should have saved her."

"I did," I say.

"Help me, Marcus!" my wife says, and I make a strange yelping sound, because her whole body is covered with gum. What Aubrey would look like if she were a cartoon character.

I yank off the wads and try to purify her, but I'm way too late to help her. Underneath the gum is a bulging eye, an open mouth, blistering flesh.

The unicorn eats a piece of gum off her cheek.

I remember the hospital. I remember shaving Aubrey's head. I remember her telling me about the baby in her dreams who she believed represented her own mortality. I remember her decision to die at home.

I wanted to save her, but I wasn't strong enough.

I let the disease kill my wife.

There's no one here to punish me for my weakness. But lucky for me, the unicorn is just the no one for the job. She gallops toward my eye, and in no time at all, I'm dreaming of hospitals.

Shots and Cuts

by
Mary Borsellino

There's almost nothing on this planet that can shove me out of my comfort zone. That was true when I was a snot-nosed kid, and after fifteen years in the homicide unit, it's even truer.

Serves me well on the job, but there's a downside.

Take last Christmas, for example. Sitting around the table after we'd picked the turkey down to scraps on a ribcage, everyone mellow and chatty, and I realise that the only topics I know anything about are tales of the bleakest places in the human soul. I start telling this one story, about the Maniacs, because that's the one I've been reading up on for a local case. Murder's like any other human interest: if you want to be an expert, you have to stay ahead of the trends.

So I mention something about the case, because I think it's quirky enough to pique at least a little interest, and my sister gives me this look that shut me right the hell up. My sister's as normal and suburban as they come — the opposite of me — and so I've started using her as my yardstick of what it's not okay to talk about at the family Christmas. Turns out the answer is pretty much 'everything I know about.'

Her kids want to hear more, of course. She's got twins, fraternal but both boys, nearly fifteen. Too smart to give much of a shit about school, too dumb to know what to do with themselves otherwise. Old enough to get away with hearing about gory shit and young enough that they can't really comprehend the full meaning of said shit. But maybe I'm not giving them enough credit there; kids grow up early, these days.

Have you been to a concert lately? Doesn't matter the band. Rock, pop, metal — same's true for them all. Next time you're at a show, look away from the stage and around at the crowd.

Little camera screens everywhere, right? Mostly cellphones, some regular cameras. But all of them digital and all of them set to video mode.

Forget any rumours of debauchery and drug use going on backstage; the real danger to the souls of rock and rollers comes from that old chestnut about cameras stealing your spirit when they capture an image. Those poor musicians have been fractured into a thousand thousand YouTube uploads.

The weird part is that most of the kids with the cameras, they aren't watching the stage. Their eyes are on their screens like they're already preparing the memory rather than living the moment. Like my sister's kids, who can't keep their phones out of their hands at the Christmas dinner table or through a movie screening. Always only halfway paying attention to the real world.

Growing up in the age of the Internet has made this younger generation into expert curators of their own lives. They all know how to angle a snapshot to make their faces thinner, how to phrase an update so their day sounds exciting and glamorous. Life stops happening and becomes how they shape the memory of it. Zoom in, jump cut, adjust the audio levels.

So what, right? If kids would rather collect a life than live it then that's their business, isn't it? Okay, sure. But remember this: a generation's monsters reflect the generation. Charles Manson turned free love into free hate. Ted Bundy keeping severed heads in his house like acquisition would lead automatically to fulfillment. Kids in black trench coats thinned locker-room herds.

If the world fears its monsters, what frightens twice as hard is the spectre of a teenage villain. Teenagers, even the non-monstrous variety, do not play by grown-up rules. They care too much about some things and not enough about others. Their emotions simmer constantly, just a degree or two short of boiling over. Even at their most placid, teenagers are *scary*. My sister's kids are still years away from learning the art of moderation, of subtlety. Everything happens to them with the volume turned up to eleven.

One last thing before I start the story of the Maniacs, something you already know if you've ever watched a crime drama on TV or read a paperback thriller you bought at the airport. One last piece to put on the board before we start the game. It's this: serial killers take trophies from their kills. A lock of hair, a drop of blood, a watchband, a shoe. Something they can keep like a holy relic of their crime. Through this trophy, the killer is able to relive the murder. Sights and sounds and memories, all locked up in one little object, tidy as a YouTube link.

I'm sure you've started to see what sort of situation all these facts could lead to, if properly combined.

In June and July of 2007, twenty-one extremely brutal murders took place in the Ukraine, in a town called Dnipropetrovsk. I'm talking some Jack the Ripper shit here, and even worse than that. Faces bludgeoned with hammers until nothing resembling a face remained. Eyes gouged out of still-living victims. A pregnant woman sliced open to cut out the fetus. Children, the elderly, the drunk and homeless. Multiple bodies turned up every day. Some had their jewellery or phones stolen, though most of them weren't even robbed.

One time, near to the start of the reign of terror — what else is there to call it, honestly — two 14-year-olds were the victims, attacked in broad daylight. One of the kids died, but the other managed to get away. The police denied him access to counsel and then beat him in an effort to make him confess to killing his friend.

Shit like that gets me really steamed. It's shitty police work, and never does anything but work in a defendant's favour when you get to trial — and that's assuming that you've got the right guy to begin with, which in this case they didn't.

Sure, sure, there's reasons like personal liberties and freedom and all that. Violating the rights of another human being is never a good idea. But even purely from a pursuit-of-justice standpoint, it's a shitty methodology to employ. Anything that's gonna muddy the waters dividing the good guys (cops) from the bad guys (mass-murdering scumbag freaks) is poor procedure, in my opinion.

Twenty-one is almost too many people to comprehend as entire individuals, alive or dead. Think of all that you are, all that you hope to be, all that you remember and love and hate. It's unfathomably large. Double that. Then add another. You're still only up to three people. To get to twenty-one, you have to multiply those three infinities by seven. Then take that sublimely huge mass of consciousness, and snuff it out. Use a piece of steel construction pipe, and strike over and over until there's nothing left but red pulp on the ice of a sidewalk.

Authorities recorded a total of twenty-nine attacks. Somewhat miraculously, eight people survived their attempted murders.

But all this is nothing more or less than the usual bloodshed of human history, is it? After all, the recent history of the Ukraine alone has also given us Andrei Chikatilo, who mutilated and murdered more than fifty children and women. Or if you want to get even more specific and stay in Dnipropetrovsk, there's the police investigator Serhiy Tkach, who confessed to murdering more than a hundred children and women.

Don't think that the Russians have something bad in the water, either. Albert Fish was born and raised in

America, and in addition to counting his total victims at over a hundred, he liked to boast that he'd raped and eaten a child in every state of the USA.

To put it bluntly, humanity produces some seriously fucked pieces of shit on a regular basis. So why am I talking about one grubby little string of not quite two dozen kills? Well, the age of the killers, for starters. All this horror and gore was generated by two teenage boys, Viktor Sayenko and Igor Suprunyuck. Nineteen-year-old kids.

They grew up together, their friendship forged by the bullying they both endured and a shared fear of heights. When they were twelve years old, the boys decided to conquer that fear in the same kind of reckless bullshit way that kids try to do all kinds of dumb stuff. They climbed over the railing on the balcony of a 14th-floor apartment and hung on, bare against the wind and gravity.

Igor and Viktor stayed there on that edge for hours, and when they finally went back inside, their fear of heights had vanished.

A third friend, Alexander, had terrors of his own: hemophobia. Crippling fear of blood.

If confronting heights had cured the two boys of their fear, Igor figured that the same logic should apply for Alexander's own terror. Why not torture stray dogs, and get used to blood that way?

I ask you, what kind of fucking logic is that?

So anyway, that's what they did. Over and over. And over. They took photos, posing in silly mustaches beside their kills, drawing graffiti with the blood. Then their rituals evolved, as killers' rituals always do. They moved on to pet cats, and they moved on to video.

The reason why I'm telling you about twenty-one sordid little murders is because these kids shot their kills in just the same way that kids at concerts do. Zoom in, jump cut, adjust the audio levels.

Upload.

Here's another little piece of info about humanity. I

should have provided it back at the beginning with the rest of the backgrounding, but like I said a minute ago, if you try to take in too much knowledge at once it all gets a little unreal. Twenty-one murders stops seeming twenty-one times more terrible than one murder. Humanity's capacity for depravity starts to lose its impact. Your nerves get dull from repeated exposure.

So here's a bonus bit of charm: '2 girls 1 cup.' That's the name of a minute-long viral video, also from 2007. Two women shit into a cup, then eat it, then vomit into each other's mouths.

What made the video famous wasn't simply the content. It was the YouTube fad which followed it, in which viewers set their webcams to record their reactions as they watched the video for the first time. Then they'd upload these reactions, showcasing horror and disgust, humor and nonchalance. The fad grew and grew — *Esquire* magazine did an article about getting George Clooney to do a reaction. Popular cartoon shows included animated gags of characters viewing the video.

A random little piece of scat porn had become the new yardstick by which everyone was measuring how jaded or innocent they were. Surely, this was the worst of the worst, the most base and foul thing anyone would ever have an opportunity to sit through.

Well, okay. Sure. Except that then, one day, a new video started going the rounds. This one quickly got the nickname '3 guys 1 hammer.'

There were Viktor and Igor and a man on the ground. There was the hammer of the title, wrapped in a plastic bag to protect it as it struck the man over and over. His name was Sergei Yatzenko. He'd recently survived throat cancer. He looked after his disabled mother. He had two children and one grandchild.

Viktor and Igor were surprised to find that Sergei was still alive, lapsing in and out of consciousness, even after they'd stabbed a screwdriver into his eye and into exposed parts of his brain.

We know they were surprised because they say so in the video, in mild and calm tones, while they wash their hands and the hammer with bottled water.

Can you even start to look for a motive in a set of actions like those of Viktor and Igor? Can deeds like that ever have an excuse or reason?

During the boys' trial, the fact emerged that Igor had been collecting newspaper clippings about his murders, annotating them in a scrapbook.

Of the videos themselves, one of the Detectives on the case offered this as an explanation: "We think they were doing it as a hobby, to have a collection of memories when they get old."

The abyss at the heart of the human soul is a deep, dark place. It's probably not wise to gaze into it for very long. I try not to, even when I'm working a case and doing my best to get inside the heads of monsters.

But they caught the monsters, so everything's okay now, right? Igor and Viktor are gonna be behind bars for the rest of their days. Their collections, horrifying though they may be, are never going to get any bigger.

Except that in April 2011, authorities arrested two more teenaged kids for six more murders in Siberia, after a video turned up of a woman's death and mutilation. This new pair used the internet to read up on the activities of the kids in Dnipropetrovsk. They were inspired, and so grabbed a mallet and a knife and a camera and set out to start their own collections.

Remember that Nicholas Cage movie from a few years back, *8mm*? In it there's a video that looks like it shows a murder, but everyone's sure it must be fake? It isn't just that they want to believe that the film is staged because they have faith in the human spirit or some shit like that — even two-dimensional characters in a gory crime thriller genuinely believe that snuff movies don't ever really exist. It seems too unfathomable, too horrible. Surely, nobody is capable of creating such a thing.

Ever hear that saying about truth being stranger than fiction? I guess we have to add 'infinitely more fucked up' to truth's attributes.

I just typed Sergei Yatzenko's name into Google to make sure I'd spelled it right, and the autocomplete option on the search bar offered me: 'sergei yatzenko video', 'sergei yatzenko death', 'sergei yatzenko killing', 'sergei yatzenko hammer', and 'sergei yatzenko YouTube'.

Forget shady back rooms and underworld deals and clandestine meetings by shadowy figures. Snuff movies are not only real, you can bring 'em up on your home computer at the click of a button.

And remember how those girls and their gross kinky little shock video inspired all those reactions? What's good for the goose turns out to be good for the gander. YouTube is now cluttered with reaction videos of people watching '3 guys 1 hammer.' The edgier message board conversations of the net use animated images of the killing strike to punctuate their banter. Murder, real murder, has become a punch line.

And I'm part of the infection too, sitting there with my family at Christmas, talking about this shit as if it's an acceptable topic of conversation for anyone, anywhere, outside of an investigation or a courtroom. Fuck it, give the world a few more years and people won't bat an eyelash when the chit-chat wanders to the subject of viral-video murder porn.

It started with three guys and a hammer. But now you have to take that three, and start multiplying. Seven times three. Seven times seven times three. Seven times seven times seven by three. Who knows how big and deep and dark that abyss can grow before it swallows everything whole.

Reaction videos will spawn reaction videos, and here and there a kid might get inspired to go a step further and add to the stockpile of the core viral load.

Articles will get written, and articles will get glued into scrapbooks.

Even these words right here that I'm typing to you are adding to the sum total, aren't they?

You and me, right now, we're part of this.

The collection's taken on a life of its own, and it's just going to keep growing and growing.

Ride

by
Brent Michael Kelley

"Let's ride," I say.

I kick my bike, Molly, to life and roar out onto the road. The man with the missing heart is dead-but-twitching in front of the smoldering gas station. Warm 9mm casings glint in the dirt next to his empty Glock. Shoot better, motherfucker.

Geezer, Robot, and the gang are right behind me, sucking my exhaust. There are only a dozen of us left. I'm certain we constitute the twelve nastiest sonsabitches left on the planet. Some of them wear flak jackets, but not me. I wear my chapter colors, some guns, and a big goddamn knife. I wear a satchel over my shoulder that's stuffed with human hearts. Body armor? Ha! Goddamn horseshit.

The black, oily clouds vomit out masses of flaming sludge. The whole goddamn sky is burning, and there's nothing anybody can do about it. A smallish fireball — maybe the size of a dog, who knows — smashes the road in front of me like a rocket.

I swerve it, skidding just a tad, getting sprayed with white-hot gravel. I hammer on the gas. I hit 120 mph, on my way to top speed. My cigar burns fast and hot, blowing a steady stream of hot, glowing ash back over my cheek.

In the mirror, I see my crew getting pulverized into flaming dust. At this point, it doesn't matter if they keep up or get smoked. They would agree.

There's a truck on its side in the ditch up ahead. I see

people seeing me, and I see them diving out of view. I signal the remaining boys that I'm stopping. We screech to a halt, and I'm off Molly in a flash. My hair trails behind me like a comet's tail as I race around the truck.

There are two men and a woman huddled up and trying to hide from me. One of the men points a shaky .38 in my general direction. I pull my knife, and I advance.

The .38 fires four times, each shot going astray. Shoot better, motherfucker. I'd laugh if it wasn't the end of the world. But then, I laugh because it *is* the end of the world.

The man is still pulling the trigger on the .38. It clicks in his hand, impotent and used up.

They struggle, but by then the boys have them pinned down. I tell them I'm doing them a favor. As I cut out their beating hearts one by one, I tell them it's better this way.

These three hot, slippery items go into the satchel with the rest, and I'm back in Molly's saddle. The blood on my arms looks black under the charred sky. With these last three, I figure the total is twenty-four.

Down the road a ways, an old man and his son have shotguns. Shoot better, motherfuckers. Hearts into the basket.

Down the road some more, there's a woman with two terrified toddlers. I leave them be, even though I'd be doing them a favor.

Down the road a little further, there's a fat man with a Desert Eagle. Shoot better, motherfucker. Heart into the basket.

I think that's twenty-seven, and I count them to be sure.

Robot has a coughing fit, then he falls over. He dies clawing at his ribs and banging his shaved head into the blacktop. Geezer and me, we don't mourn him. We ain't far behind.

Geezer has a coughing fit of his own. When it's over, he nods to me. I nod back. He walks off a ways, and, even though I know what he's going to do, I watch. He draws his sidearm, and I hear the crack of the gunshot. His head snaps sideways, and his whole body jerks. As he falls to the ground, his hands flail for something that isn't there. Geezer's gone, replaced by a pile of twitching meat.

I count exactly twenty-seven hearts. Perfect.

When I roll up to the edge of the cliff where you're buried, I'm alone with the boiling, black clouds. The sound of the world dying is so loud I'm amazed I'm not deaf yet. It's like all the jet engines in the world are blasting in my ears while the Devil stabs icepicks into my eardrums. I can feel blood trickling from them.

Your grave is marked by the handlebars of your motorcycle. I pour some whiskey for you, then I take down the rest of the bottle. When it's gone, I throw it in the air and blast it to hell with my new Desert Eagle.

I empty the bag of hearts on the ground over your body. Twenty-seven of them. One for every year of your life. One for every year I loved you. My kid brother. The one I taught to catch fireflies, and then to smear them on his clothes. The kid brother who I taught to ride a bicycle. Who I taught to ride a real bike five years later. Who went to the grave trying to be like me, when my only wish was to be more like him. The kid brother I wish I could have died instead of.

With gas siphoned from Molly, I set the hearts on fire. I don't know what it means, this burnt offering, this human sacrifice. Maybe I only wanted to share the pain, the agony of having my heart torn out. In any case, it's done. In any case, I did it for you.

Up above, there's another fireball coming. A big one. The kind that it don't matter if a guy runs. With a cold smile, I touch your handlebar.

"Let's ride," I say.

Mrs. Grainger's Animal Emporium

by
Phil Hickes

An autumn day in the small English town of Malreward is coming to an end. The sun writes a spectacular farewell note across the sky in letters of scarlet and gold. In the air is the November perfume of bonfires, frost and forgotten apples left to rot in the long grass of the orchards. Slowly, the fiery horizon cools, and inky, blue night clouds begin to gather menacingly. The wind picks up, hurrying leaves along the gutter like an impatient innkeeper ushering customers out into the night. The breeze carries the threat of winter, and the citizens of the town shudder and pull wooly scarves tight around their necks. They rush to get home, eager to be settled in front of a crackling fire with hot tea and buttered toast. It's not a night to be outside, particularly at this strange time of year, when twigs in the hedgerows snap without reason, and cold fingers tap at the windows.

A young boy with untidy brown hair and small, mean eyes is dawdling outside a shop. He leans forward against the window and cups his hands over his face. As he breathes out, a small circle of glass steams up, and he quickly wipes it with the grubby sleeve of his jacket, leaving behind a greasy smear. The shop fascinates him. In a town where nothing much happens, a new shop is an exciting event and well worth investigating. But this one is even more intriguing because of the sign above it. It's written in fancy black letters, the ends of which swoop and swirl enticingly like eyelashes, and say:

MRS GRAINGER'S ANIMAL EMPORIUM.

The young boy with mean eyes wonders what an 'Animal Emporium' could be. It sounds exciting and exotic. He imagines that it's a place where rare and dangerous animals are housed, before being sold off to rich collectors. That would be perfect. In his mind, he sees himself feeding mice to coiled pythons, watching the thick, scaly limbs slowly wrap themselves around their terrified prey. Or there might be a tank of piranha fish, and he can drop his sister's gerbil into the churning water and see how long it takes those needle teeth to strip it to the bone. Maybe there'll be some talking parakeets, and he can teach them to screech 'piss off!' at the customers.

All of this runs through his mind as he deliberately slides his nose slowly down the window, leaving a snail trail of snot. He's angry because there's nothing to see. Heavy, red velvet curtains are drawn inside the windows, shutting out even the nosiest of parkers. The door is locked (he's tried it). And just in case anyone is still unsure, there's a lopsided sign hanging in the doorway which declares that the shop is CLOSED. Hands stuck deep in his coat pockets, he reluctantly turns and heads for home, but not before aiming two kicks at the door. Satisfied with this act of revenge, he turns and snorts, before hawking out a great globule of phlegm at a passing pigeon, which waddles away nervously.

At that moment, there is a quiet click from behind him.

The small boy turns and his mean eyes narrow suspiciously, which make them look even meaner, if that were possible.

The door that was locked shut is now slightly ajar, revealing a slice of inviting blackness. What's more, the sign has changed its mind and now says *OPEN*. It's strange, and he waits to see if anyone appears. Despite his impatience to see what lies behind the door, there is a slight churning in his stomach. It feels like the time when he ate a green cooking apple for a dare and it made him sick. Why would the shop open when everything else is closing? For some reason, he imagined the mayor of the town would come and cut a red ribbon with a large pair of scissors, and everybody would clap before wandering in to have a look.

Still....

He takes a step closer.

He knows that he really should be getting home to have his tea. His mother will be stirring something hot on the stove, waiting to ask him if he's done his homework (he hasn't). His dad will be busy reading *The Sun* in the front room. Upstairs, his stupid sister will be dancing around her room to the rubbish boy band music she constantly plays.

Five minutes won't make any difference.

Just a quick look to satisfy his curiosity.

He walks towards the door, pauses, then pushes it and goes in.

The heavy, velvet curtains swing into his face. Angrily, he sweeps them out of the way. They smell of dust and age. Like a prayer book in an old church.

Then he stands in silent amazement.

In front of him is a zoo that's been frozen in time.

Covering every available space, are hundreds and hundreds of stuffed animals and birds. It's the largest collection of anything that he's ever seen — and that includes Wayne Ashworth's collection of dirty magazines. It's hard to know where to look first.

As his gaze travels around the shop, he sees glass cases containing all sorts of weird and wonderful creatures. In one is a snarling fox. In another, two owls stare back at him with wide orange eyes. There is a solitary magpie, and he quickly touches his forehead to avert bad luck. Another contains five or six brightly coloured tropical birds, some in mid-flight. Hanging around the tops of the walls are the heads of deer, antelopes, wild boars and goats, and the boy lingers with delight on their wicked looking horns and tusks.

But there's more to see.

Over to his right are lines of shelves, each one laden with curiosities. A cross-eyed rabbit flees an unseen predator. A shocked looking green woodpecker pauses mid-peck. On a lower shelf stands a huge, funny looking bird-duck thing. It looks familiar. The cogs whirr. It's a Dodo! He read about them once, and how they were hunted down by men with guns. Every single one. Seeing one up close he's not surprised — they look slow and stupid. He raises an imaginary rifle to his shoulder and completes the genocide with a whispered, "Bang."

Everything has a label and a price-tag, and he shuffles forward to read the names of the animals and birds he doesn't recognize: there is a cormorant; an oyster catcher; a razorbill and plover; a pair of mergansers; a nightjar; something called a glossy ibis, which has an incredibly long and sharp beak; a fierce silver mink; a shrew; a growling pine martin and an ermine stoat.

His attention then is drawn by a little family of rats. They're arranged on top of a circular piece of wood, to which a few plastic twigs and leaves have been added for effect. The foliage doesn't look very realistic. Besides, everyone knows that rats live in sewers, so it's doubly stupid. He's always wanted a rat, but his parents have told him that he can't have one because they're unhygienic. It's so unfair.

He glances around the shop. He's still alone. Slowly he reaches for one of the rats and strokes it, feeling its coarse black hairs under his fingers. He draws his finger against its long front teeth, which still feel ripe for tearing. There are so many animals in here that it's impossible anyone will notice one is missing. And it's small. And it's not like it's the only one. Mind made up, he quickly yanks it free from its flimsy mooring before opening his school bag and popping it inside. He's already thinking of leaving it in his sister's bed. His mean eyes narrow and he checks to see if he's being observed by security cameras.

Nothing.

And then his thudding heart thuds a little faster.

At the back of the shop, he sees what looks like a small wildcat of some kind. And there's a chimpanzee. And next to it an orangutan. Between them, a human skeleton dangles from a wire. There's one in the science laboratory at school, though he doesn't think it's real. The bones on this one have an unpleasant yellow tinge, like a skeleton of a Roman soldier he saw in a museum once. Maybe this one is real, too. Oddly, someone's placed a top hat on its head. It looks like a posh dinner guest whose food never arrived. And then he notices that dotted among the animals and birds on the shelves there are two or three detached human skulls, which makes it feel as though he's wandered into the lair of a sorcerer or a witch.

This is the best place that he has ever visited in his life. And that includes Euro Disney.

There's hardly any space to move within the shop, but he edges closer to the shelf to have a look at one of the skulls. Nervously, he stretches out a hand and places it on top of what he assumes was once someone's head. It feels smooth and surprisingly delicate, as though he could crack it with his fingers. He squeezes it a little tighter.

A voice crackles like an old record.

"I'd rather you didn't touch the collection unless you're going to buy — are you going to buy?"

The boy turns. For a second, he thought the skull was talking to him. But then he looks around and notices a small silhouette standing at the back of the shop. The figure steps forward, and he sees that it is a tiny old woman. She's even smaller than his sister, who's only ten years old. This lady looks one hundred and ten.

The small lady is frowning as she ambles up to him. Her hair is thinning and that odd bluey-violet colour that you sometimes see on old English ladies. She wears thick glasses with purple frames, behind which are tiny black eyes set in a pudgy, wrinkled face that droops at the sides. The boy thinks she looks like a fruitcake mix before it goes in the oven. A smirk forms on his lips. This little old lady isn't going to give him any trouble.

"Just looking," he says, leaving his hand on the skull.

"Yes, well, that skull once belonged to someone who was just looking, too," she says frostily.

He moves his hand away.

She inches a little closer and the boy notices a strong odor, a blend of lavender and bleach. It reminds him of the hospital corridor where he waited for his grandfather to die.

Unconsciously, he moves backwards to the door, his feet knocking into something as he does so. He turns to see a weasel staring up at him, its sharp front teeth poised to bite.

"Please watch where you're stepping, young man," the old lady crackles, "any damages will have to be paid for."

"Yeah, well, I'm done looking and now I'm going," he says. He wants to get away from this smelly dwarf lady and get the rat safely back home. Maybe cut it open and see what's inside.

She comes closer. The dim light catches her glasses so that her eyes become silver crescents in the gloom of the shop. Her voice drops to a whisper.

"I do hope you're not one of those boys that like to take things that don't belong to them — are you?" The little lady peers intently at him.

The boy feels his face redden and his temper rise.

"I wouldn't take anything from here, it's just a load of dead animals," he snarls.

The old lady smiles with her mouth, but her eyes remain cold and penetrating.

"Dead you say?"

For a second, the boy sees a bat flapping towards him out of the darkness, its eyes glinting hungrily. He raises his arms and cries out. The little old lady chuckles, and the boy looks again to see that the bat is simply like all the other animals — still, silent and stuffed.

"Why, whatever's the matter with you?" she says. "You look like you've seen a ghost."

For once, he's unable to think of a smart response. Instead, he turns and stomps through the door, but not before reaching out a hand and flicking a red squirrel onto the floor, which does a stiff, forward roll before landing in an ungainly heap.

As he runs up the street, he hears a shriek that chills his bones faster than the cold night air.

* * *

Nighttime brings silence to the town. There are no drunken teenagers shouting obscenities from tatty bus shelters, or courting couples laughing as they fumble for car keys. The narrow streets are quiet and empty. Even the ubiquitous taxi driver is nowhere to be seen and has gone elsewhere to conduct his solitary vigil. Doors are locked early. Curtains are pulled tight, shutting out the darkness like an unwelcome relative. People huddle down in front of the TV and turn up the volume, lest any strange night noises have to be investigated.

But all is not as quiet as it may seem.

In one house, just a little way out of town, there is a muffled scream as a young girl finds a dead rat on her pillow. It's followed by a nasty giggle, an angry accusation and a weary appeal for peace and quiet.

Back in the high street, murmurs come from inside a shop, recently opened. Behind thick, velvet curtains, a tiny silhouette stands with hands on hips. You might think it a little girl, until you hear the gravelly croak that can only belong to someone much, much older. The figure begins to wander up and down, occasionally stopping to pat a head, tickle an ear or stroke a feather.

"And you saw him take it, did you? And you, too? Oh, you clever things. Yes, yes, I agree. He had that look about him, didn't he? You can always spot them, can't you, the rotten apples? Well, my lovelies, what are we to do?"

The small silhouette turns to the back of the shop and speaks.

"Mr. Fitzsimon, I believe this is a situation that would benefit from your... skill in these matters. Would you care to take the night air and see what can be done?"

Who, or what, she addresses doesn't reply.

But a second or two later, there is an odd clunking sound, like tuneless keys on a dead piano.

* * *

Old Fred Parnell looks up at the starry sky and feels the world revolving slowly on its axis. He staggers backwards and just manages to place a steadying hand on his front gate before becoming intimate with the pavement. Tonight he's overdone it, even by his red-faced standards. Since lunchtime, he's been settled in the snug at the Fox & Hounds, marking out his betting slip with a copy of *The Racing Post* and a pint of Bishop's Finger. And then another pint. And another. Then it was one more... oh go on, if you're buying... right, I'll have the same again... maybe a small nip... oh all right, just to keep out the cold... right, last one for me... aye go on then... God blesh ya....

... until the world dissolved like a sugar cube in a glass of Absinthe.

Now he aims his shriveled penis at the back wall of his house, before unleashing a dribble of industrial-strength urine down the front of his trousers. Oh shit. He's glad his Gladys isn't around to see him in this state; she'd turn in her grave. Melancholy descends like an autumnal mist, and as he fumbles with his zip, a solitary tear trickles over the broken veins on his cheek.

As he attempts to insert his key in the lock on his front door, which appears to be moving in a clockwise motion, he hears a clicking sound coming down the high street towards him. He turns and peers down the path, closing one eye in an effort to focus on the cone of light that hangs from the streetlamp. Into view walks a skeleton, which raises its top hat in a friendly greeting as it passes. Fred waves weakly, before inserting his key smoothly into the lock, opening the door, and slamming it shut in his most agile movement of the evening.

Fred never touches a drop again.

* * *

Police Sergeant Dave Williamson has his feet up on the desk and is reading the sports pages in the local paper when a call comes in. It's Mrs. Miller from Grange Street, ringing to tell him that she's just spotted a chimpanzee swinging from her pear tree. Sighing, he hangs up and swings his feet back up on the desk.

Bloody nightshift.

* * *

The dog is barking furiously, and Julie Henderson bites her nails as she peers out of the window. Tyson isn't a neurotic dog by any standards and only barks when he has good reason to. His yelps are like the phone ringing in the middle of the night — an unwelcome herald of dark tidings. Outside all is quiet, but in her mind, Julie sees a white hand in the bushes holding a knife. She shivers. It's at times like this that she wishes she was still married. Tyson jumps up at the door and growls, a gossamer thread of drool dangling from his jaws. Julie cringes as the spittle spirals down onto her nice, clean floor. Canine security comes at a cost. Now he's scrabbling frantically at the door, his blunt nails adding another few welts to the crisscross pattern on the paintwork. Keeping an eye out for boiler-suit-clad madmen with axes, she unlocks the door. Tyson hurriedly squeezes past her and rushes outside before the door is fully opened. She stands on the doorstep, hugging herself like a fisherman's wife awaiting news of a shipwreck.

A scrabbling in the bushes.

Tyson barks.

It's answered with a deep, guttural growl from something that doesn't wear a collar and doesn't come when it's told.

Tyson retreats, trotting quickly back into the house with his head hung, ashamed that he's failed to meet the only requirement of his job description.

Julie just wants to get the door locked again as quickly as possible.

They return upstairs and huddle on the bed together, clutching the quilt like drowning sailors clinging to a lifebelt.

Both of them are happy to forget that they ever saw something with fangs at the bottom of the garden.

* * *

Many find sleep hard to come by. It's an eerie night, punctuated by screeches and growls, hoots and yowls. People stand at their windows, considering whether they really did see a penguin waddle across their front lawn. And whilst it's not unusual to see the odd owl fly across town on a midnight hunt, it's rare to see five of them flying in formation with a golden eagle, a painted snipe and an Indian green pigeon. The citizens sigh and return to the warmth of their beds, happy to ascribe their sightings to seasonal vagaries. Perhaps even to a morsel of badly digested cheese, as that famous miser once did when haunted by ghosts.

One boy has no trouble sleeping. He's had a good day. One rat acquired. One sister freaked out. Not a bad tally all told. While younger boys clutch teddy bears to their chest, he clutches his new vermin capture, his rest deep and dreamless. He's so sound asleep that he doesn't hear the snarling and snorting of strange animals outside his window. Nor does he hear his bedroom door open. The thick carpet muffles the sound of the fleshless feet that tip toe in. The rat stirs in the boy's grip and wriggles free, greeting someone, or something, with a twitch of its whiskers and a flick of its pale worm-like tail. It scampers up and sniffs at the boy's face, wrinkling its tiny nose in what appears to be distaste. Then those long yellow teeth open and gently fasten onto the boy's fleshy upper lip. Only now does the boy stir. At first he whimpers in pain. Then, as he sees a grinning skull looking down at him, he whimpers with fear.

Then, for the next hour or so, he whimpers from a

combination of both.

* * *

A rat crouches on a pillow and licks freshly spilt blood from a bony finger.

* * *

A red-tailed hawk perches at the end of a bed and tears gooey strings of scarlet liver with its beak.

* * *

A polecat studies a tube of grey intestine which has been thrown onto a bedroom floor, before gnawing at it casually, like a stick of blueberry chewing gum.

* * *

The sun returns, a bright yellow broom here to sweep all the nasty night terrors back under the carpet. Even so, it remains a subdued start to the day, with many people lost in their thoughts, the firm pillars of normality having shifted overnight.

An old man with a red face winces as he swigs down a fizzing glass of aspirin tablets.

An attractive middle-aged lady watches a Doberman sniffing excitedly around a willow tree in her back garden.

A policeman curses as he spills tomato ketchup from his bacon sandwich onto a report of curious events.

In one house, a mother is delighted to be greeted by a hug and a kiss from her son, who is normally sullen and uncommunicative. The boy apologises to his sister, and asks if he can help with the breakfast dishes. The mother thinks he looks a little pale and asks if he's feeling okay, but he assures her that everything is wonderful, before packing his peanut butter sandwiches into his school bag and setting off for school humming a cheery pop song. The mother shrugs to herself, before fetching a dustpan and brush to clear a trail of sawdust that the boy has left on the kitchen floor. Ah well. Polite, happy and tidy would have been too much to ask.

* * *

As the town awakens, and the sun roots out any lingering shadows from the narrow streets, one place remains dark and still, resisting the day's cheery bustle. The shop that was briefly open is now closed again, its curtains drawn and door locked. Inside, a baggy faced old lady dusts her collection of animals, birds and bones. She's spent the night preparing for a new addition to her collection, and now eagerly awaits its arrival. The back door opens, and she hears slow, clumping footsteps approach. Without breaking from her task, she addresses the newcomer in her crackly voice.

"Well, well, and look what the cat dragged in. And how are you today, young man? Did you enjoy meeting Mr. Fitzsimon last night?"

A small boy stands staring blankly into space. His voice is slow, and he stumbles over his words as though someone has slipped a little Belladonna in his tea.

"I very much... enjoyed... meeting... I... pleasure... I'm so tired," he yawns.

"Hush now, you foolish boy, you're talking utter nonsense."

She turns and looks at him, her glasses a second pair of disapproving eyes.

The boy tries again. He feels so tired, as though he could lie down right now and sleep forever.

"I am... pleased... meeting... thank you very much... can I have a biscuit?"

A thin trail of sawdust trickles down between the boy's legs. He stares without seeing, his eyes glazed, lifeless and no longer quite so mean. The old lady slaps him on the cheek, the sharp thwack of flesh on flesh making him blink rapidly.

"Tsh, look at the mess you're making on my floor. Turn around and pull up your shirt, you dirty little boy!"

The boy turns, pauses, then turns again, the movement clumsy and confused. The little old lady yanks up his shirt angrily, exposing a crude line of thick, canvas stitches holding the skin of his bloodied back together. A couple of them have come loose. Sawdust pours out between his pink ribs like sand through an hourglass.

"Oh Mr. Fitzsimon, such a shoddy job!" the old lady says to a bony figure at the back of the shop. "Well, we'll have to do a little tidying before you go on show. Who on earth's going to want to buy you?"

And with that, she ushers the boy through to the back room, returning to collect a sharp butcher's knife and a thin steel needle with a hook on the end. Yes, he'll need to stay out back with the others whilst she scrapes all that sticky flesh from the bones. She doesn't want to scare any customers away, particularly the young boy in the baseball cap that's outside shoving dog dirt through her letterbox.

The Tick-Tock Heart

by
L.S. Murphy

For thirty-one years, Kate Tucker lived on Westline Drive on the north side of Carterville's town square. When she was a child, her parents owned the dry cleaners beneath their apartment. Now it was an antique shop that managed to make Kate enough money to live on. It helped that she owned the building and didn't have a mortgage or children.

But she had her tick-tocks. The wide assortment of clocks covered every wall, corner, and anywhere in between of the three bedroom townhouse apartment. In the antique shop, there were even more. When Kate needed to or could bear to part with one of her precious clocks, she would sell it. Most of her income came from internet deals, but occasionally a lost tourist would wander in and buy something.

When the little bell over the door dinged on the dreary Thursday afternoon, Kate stared into the face of the last person she ever expected to see in Carterville again. Meredith Tucker-Harper stood a step inside the door with her dirty blonde hair dripping the rain-snow mix that spit from the sky.

"Hey, Katie." Meredith didn't move, and Kate saw water begin to pool on her hardwood floor. It was just like Meredith to stand on the floor instead of the rug. "I'm home."

"What're you doing here?" Katie continued to stare at

the growing puddles. Her fingers itched to grab the mop she kept behind her desk for moments like this.

"Nice to see you too, sis," Meredith snapped. "Are you going to invite me in or do you expect me to stand here all day?"

"It's three in the afternoon."

"So?"

"The day's almost over."

Meredith shook her head and laughed.

Kate didn't see what was so funny. Especially since Meredith was now spraying the books on display in the window. Kate walked over to the front door and locked it, flipping the sign to closed. Her eyes never left her sister's face.

"You never answered my question, Meredith." The loud click of the deadbolt echoed through the tension. Kate turned to face her sister. "Why are you here?"

"Can't a girl come see her sister?" Meredith shifted, and Kate noticed the luggage on the floor.

"No, not you." Kate walked toward her desk and stopped at the steps that led up to her apartment. Over her shoulder, she sighed and asked, "Are you coming?"

Meredith's too high heels clicked rapid as the pilot case wheeled across the floor. "Thanks, Katie. I promise I'll only be here tonight."

Kate felt her heart lurch and her hand instinctively fell between her breasts. Meredith ran past her up the stairs, not noticing Kate steadying herself. It had been like this since the surgery eleven years ago. Once Kate had the pacemaker put in her heart, Meredith stopped noticing anything that Kate did. Kate was twenty and Meredith had turned sixteen a week before the surgery. Their lives went in different directions.

The clocks welcomed Kate up the stairs with their steady rhythm. It took effort, but Kate managed to keep their ticking synched. If one was off, she knew it, found it, and fixed it. The sound soothed her.

"God, Katie, I knew you had a thing for clocks, but really?" Meredith dropped her suitcase in the foyer at the top of the stairs. She pressed her hands to her ears. It looked like she smelled something horrible by the way her nose wrinkled. "I mean, do you even *know* what color the walls are?"

Kate brushed by her and continued to the kitchen. Every day at three, she made a cup of tea and sat at the small table with a book. While she knew that the peace and quiet of reading would be impossible, Kate still wanted her Oolong blend. Meredith followed her, still complaining about what she said was noise. Kate took a teacup and saucer from the cabinet. She paused and brought out another set for Meredith. Her mother would expect Kate to be cordial even if she wasn't here to see what went on between the two sisters.

""How can you stand the noise?" Meredith asked as she sat in Kate's chair at the table.

Kate filled the kettle. "I've lived with it for eleven years."

"Oh," Meredith huffed.

"You still haven't told me why you've come." Kate kept her back to Meredith as she adjusted the heat on the stove. Slow-boiled water made the best tea, in her opinion. Just because her sister interrupted her carefully constructed life didn't mean she should change her routine.

"Cale kicked me out last night." Meredith sounded neither upset or surprised as she announced this news.

"Why?" Kate walked to the table, momentarily forgetting that Meredith was in her seat. She stopped and then took the chair across from her sister. "Why would he kick you out for no reason?"

Meredith stared out the little window. The sun broke through the clouds and bathed her in a golden glow. It suited her. Meredith was the golden child of the family. She was the cheerleader, the scholarship winner, the perfect girlfriend then wife. Meredith could do nothing wrong. Kate had a bad heart and cost the family most of their savings.

"He found out about Rodney," Meredith stated as if Kate should already know who he was.

She didn't. "Who's Rodney?"

A smile played at her sister's lips. "Rodney is... everything Cale isn't. He's smart, funny, and passionate." She sighed, letting the smile spread across her face. "Oh is he passionate." She paused, and Kate sensed her sister was remembering something she herself could never imagine. "Anyway," Meredith said as she broke from her reverie, "Cale came home early. Rodney was still getting dressed when Cale found us in the bedroom. As I'm sure you can figure, I was still naked on the bed. So, here I am."

"Why would you do that to Cale? You've been together since you were freshmen in high school." Confusion clouded Kate's mind. *Why would anyone cheat on the person they'd devoted their life to?*

"Cale was boring. I needed more than the same old life." Meredith laughed.

Kate's shock was mimicked by the teakettle whistling. She hurried to the stove to steep her tea and forgot to offer her sister any. Then again, she didn't think Meredith deserved it at the moment.

"I just need a place to stay tonight, Katie. Then I'll be out of your hair, okay?" Meredith stood and stretched her arms over her head. "If you don't mind, I'm going to lay down for a nap. I've been driving for four and a half hours. I'm totally beat."

All Kate could do was nod. Every romance novel she had ever read never compared to what she saw between her sister and brother-in-law. They were always touching one another, holding hands, stealing looks. It seemed wrong that Meredith would suddenly throw her marriage away for a tryst. She shook the thoughts from her mind. It was none of her business, and she had other things to worry about.

While Meredith rested, Kate packaged up her online sales from the day and walked two blocks to the post office. She also added an additional stop at the grocery store to get dinner. Meredith's arrival thwarted Kate's intention of eating leftovers. Their mother taught them to be respectful and to serve unwanted guests as they would invited guests. Kate had no idea what Meredith would eat, so she bought the few things she would need for potato soup. On a gloomy evening, soup was exactly what Kate thought was appropriate.

When she climbed the back steps to her apartment, Kate heard it. A clock was out of sync. It ticked when it should've tocked. After dinner, she would listen until she found it, and then it would be off to the spare room where she kept the tools and parts.

Meredith walked into the kitchen as Kate finished boiling the potatoes. The off-beat ricocheted in Kate's head, but she tried not to let it bother her.

"Is that Mom's recipe?" Meredith asked as she closed her eyes and inhaled the smell of cream and chives that simmered in a small pot. She sat at the table, lost in a memory. "It was always my favorite. Remember how she used to make it whenever either one of us was sick."

Kate nodded but didn't answer. Their mother made the soup for two weeks straight after Kate returned from the hospital with her new pacemaker. After that, their mother rarely cooked the soup even when either girl would beg for it. Kate made it for the funeral six years ago after their parents were killed in a car accident.

"Then you got sick..." Meredith let the accusation trail off. It was the same old story, and Kate had heard it all before. Meredith's problems were Kate's fault. Like Kate planned on having a heart attack when she was twenty.

The silence filled the room and the ailing clock grew louder. She tried to figure out what made it so erratic. It sped up in the last few minutes and was now slowing down to the earlier off-beat.

Meredith chatted about anything and everything that came to mind while Kate finished the soup. Not once did Meredith ask her sister about her life. Nor did Kate expect her too. Still, she thought it would be nice. Not that Kate heard what Meredith was saying anyway. Her ears were fine-tuned to the clock. It was so loud that it had to be somewhere in the kitchen.

As soon as dinner ended, Meredith excused herself to the living room and turned on the TV. Kate began her search. The most likely culprit was the cute kitty clock near the back door that had been the most recently repaired. She closed her eyes and pressed her ear to its belly. The clock tick-tocked slow and steady, perfectly in time with the rest of the house. Kate proceeded to the cuckoo clock. It was also in sync with the normal rhythm.

After an hour and a half, Kate determined that the ailing timepiece was not in the kitchen. It was nearly eight when she joined Meredith on the couch. Her sister had turned on some horrible reality show where women do useless things to impress a man. Meredith didn't even notice, or at least acknowledge, Kate's presence.

But the clock called for her help.

She stood and meticulously went from clock to clock, seeking out the traitorous rhythm. None of the clocks were injured. Not the large grandfather that occupied the wall between the two windows. Not the three mantel clocks that sat above the fireplace.

"What're you doing?" Meredith peered over the back of the couch as Kate slipped between it and the wall.

"One of my clocks is off," Kate replied as if that should explain it all.

"Off?" Meredith turned around and perched on the couch like a puppy dog. She reached out, taking down a small Swiss clock and putting it to her ear. "Sounds good to me. Why don't you sit back down and watch this show? You can figure out which clock is off later. It's not like it's the end of the world." At that, Meredith turned and slumped back onto the couch with her usual dramatic flourish.

"You wouldn't understand," Kate mumbled to her sister. To her clocks, she said, "But you do."

When the search behind the couch yielded no results, Kate stood in the middle of the room and listened. First, she focused on her own ticker. The pacemaker's steady rhythm clicked inside her chest. Once she was certain it wasn't her heart that was out of tune, Kate focused on the sound that was disrupting her evening.

Thud, thud. Thud, thud.

It sounded like a hammer hitting something organic. There was only one organic clock in the house. Kate hurried to the hallway where she checked the sound of her potato clock. Upon first inspection, she saw that the spuds were wilting. She listened, and sure enough, the clock's tick was slower than its tock. Relieved to have found the problem, Kate changed the potatoes and reset the clock to the correct rhythm.

She smiled as she stared at it, feeling the world was right once again. Without a word to Meredith, Kate went to her room to sleep off the panic that tried to consume her. She fell asleep within moments of lying down, the tick-tocks lulling her by beating along with her own heart.

It was almost two in the morning when Kate woke in a sweat. Panic seized her, making her heart beat out of time. She didn't remember any dream, good or bad. The last time she'd woken up with such a start, one of her clocks had tick-tocked a slow death.

But she checked the entire apartment earlier, and they were all fine.

She closed her eyes and counted the ticks and tocks until her heart matched the rhythm of the house. Then she heard it. The steady thumping beat out of sync again. It was the same as earlier. Kate climbed out of bed, fixated on the off beat. She closed her eyes and let the sound bring her to it.

Her toes crested the top of the steps. Carefully, she

reached for the banister and took each step down all thirteen stairs. She didn't open her eyes but knew she was on the right track. The thump-thump ricocheted off the walls.

It was close.

She used her hand to feel her way down the hall to the spare room. Meredith was asleep inside it, but that's where the ailing clock was. Kate took a deep breath, promising herself to be as quiet as possible as she searched.

The doorknob was cool beneath her touch. She opened her eyes as she pushed the door open. The shades were closed, blocking out all the light from the alley. Meredith didn't move or acknowledge this blatant lack of privacy. Kate felt ashamed for the first time since their parents died. It wasn't right to enter the room where her sister was sleeping. But it also wasn't right that Meredith showed up out of nowhere, asking a place to stay.

Kate bucked up the courage and closed her eyes once more. The thump-thump reverberated in her chest. Yes, she was in the right room. She circled the bed, seeking the clock. Each one she touched ticked the right beat. As she made her way around the room, she grew concerned. It was in this room. That was certain.

Yet each clock seemed to be their usual fine-tuned selves.

Once again, Kate closed her eyes. The thumping grew louder as she refocused. With her hands in front of her, she tentatively stepped through the room. Her shin smacked the bed rail. It took great effort not to cry out, but she managed it.

When she opened her eyes, Meredith rolled over. The thumping grew louder. Kate stared at her sister's chest. The beat was Meredith's heart.

Relief filled Kate from head to toe. She didn't have an ailing clock. Her sister was the one out of sync with the rest of them. Kate almost laughed out loud. The problem would remedy itself the next day. Nothing would have to be done. Nothing needed repaired. Nothing was broken.

Kate shuffled down the hall, up the stairs, and collapsed in her bed.

She lay there, staring at the ceiling as the thump-thump kept her awake.

One sleepless night was okay. Meredith said she'd be gone the next day.

* * *

Three days later, Meredith still had not left. Kate's patience disappeared after the second night, but she couldn't kick her sister out. Her mother taught Kate to be kind, and she would honor that memory. Even if Meredith was doing everything she could to drive Kate insane.

It was worse at night. The erratic thumping of Meredith's heart kept Kate awake. Kate's eyes were red and swollen, burning from the lack of sleep. She called the doctor and he fit her in for a quick appointment. She came home with a prescription of sleeping pills.

When she walked through the front door of the shop, which Meredith promised to watch, Kate almost lost what little lunch she had eaten. The walls were covered with her precious clocks. And they were all off the normal rhythm.

"Hey, Katie," Meredith said cheerfully as she walked down the stairs, dragging the smaller grandfather clock behind her. "I thought we could sell these now that I'm home. I mean, they are driving me up the wall with all their ticking and tocking."

Kate barely heard her. All she could focus on was the sound that the clock made as Meredith pulled it down the stairs. It screamed in agony as it bumped against the banister from Meredith's hippy walk.

"And since I'll be staying awhile, it would be nice to have my old room back." Meredith sat the clock down rougher than necessary and pushed it against the far wall. "So I started putting your tools in a box." She turned and smiled at Kate. "I hope you don't mind."

The world started to cave in on Kate. Her heart sped up, and her chest felt like it was caving in. She stared at the floor, and calmly replied, "It's fine."

But it wasn't fine. She knew it, and Meredith knew it. Kate walked up the stairs like she had these last several years, each foot in time with her heart. She went into her small workroom, Meredith's old bedroom, and began gathering her things on the table. She kept hearing everything out of sync, even though the floor was between her and her tick-tocks. She heard them moaning out of time, ailing that their precision was gone. As she stood over the table, she found the one project she'd worked on for years.

A tick-tock heart.

Kate made it when she believed her pacemaker was giving out on her. It was meant to replace the tissue in her chest when it finally, inevitably failed. She held the heart in the palm of her hand. Now she knew it was never truly meant for her.

Without thinking about the consequences, Kate sat on her stool and began working on the tick-tock heart. In the time it takes to wind a watch, the heart was running. Kate smiled and held it close to her eye. She could see the gears moving, clicking together. Ticking. Tocking.

After cleaning up the rest of the parts, Kate took her things to her room and stashed the tick-tock heart in the pocket of her sweater coat. The plan formed as she entered the kitchen and saw her sleeping pills sitting on the counter.

Dinner was a quiet affair. Meredith was too exhausted to talk. Kate was grateful for that fact, although the reason she was exhausted was because she moved all of Kate's beloved clocks to the shop. One of which, the largest of the mantle clocks with the cherry wood base, Meredith sold for a mere fifty dollars. The thought of that clock on another mantle made Kate sick to her stomach. She didn't eat much of the chicken noodle soup she had made from scratch.

"I'm so tired," Meredith complained as soon as she finished her second bowl. "What is it about soup that always does this to me?"

"I don't know," Kate responded. She hid the little smirk that crept onto her face. "Maybe it's all the moving you did today."

"True." Meredith stretched her arms over her head and then stood. "I'll put this away for you, okay?"

Kate watched as Meredith poured the remainder of the soup into a bowl. She saw Meredith look at the empty bottle of pills that Kate's doctor had prescribed. She noted the realization in her sister's eyes. She stared at Meredith's lips as they asked Kate why.

She smiled as Meredith lost consciousness and fell onto the floor.

Kate stood from her chair and knelt over her sister's supine form. The smile never left her face as she stared at a peaceful Meredith.

"It'll be okay," Kate whispered as she pulled the tick-tock heart from her pocket. She pulled a long thin knife from the butcher block on the counter. "I'll make it all right."

She placed the tick-tock heart on the floor and then slid the knife into her sister's chest.

Arkitektur

by
Michael R. Colangelo

There's something wrong with the house.

Pretty wallpaper, yes. Mother upstairs in the attic building her dolls quietly. Her hands move for themselves. Her mind has long vacated her age-ravaged body. But she still retains patterns. Retains enough dreaming to go through the motions and build her dolls up there all day and night as if no one else exists. And they don't. Not for Mother. Nothing exists but patterns. And color, sometimes. On good days, there is color too.

The wallpaper has some color to it. More important are the patterns. Sometimes little fleur-de-lis, sometimes tiny flowers. Maybe stripes, maybe checks, maybe diamonds. Gold, blue, black, silver, and a kind of yellowing crème that's curdled like the milk inside the oft-forgotten fridge buried deep in the always forgotten kitchen.

But there are other patterns too. Patterns behind the patterns on the wallpaper. These are always black and grow like creeping spider webs unseen throughout the whole house. They spawn up from the vastness underneath the house. Spores or mold or fungus or whatever one must name things to retain some footing in this world. Mother has forgotten the names of these things already anyway.

Unlike the wallpaper, these patterns move through the dark and stretch up through the basement and seep into foundations and wooden beams and carpet fibers. It creeps everywhere else too — all but blotting out an old family portrait that hangs above the fireplace mantle. In better days Mother would have thrown it out. These are not better days of course. These days are the worst.

It has been a long time. They say that isolation and murder bring a type of madness to people that they must live with or forget altogether. Mother has chosen the latter, although she can no longer bear the sight of a bottle of sleeping medication, or an axe, or a shovel and pickaxe. She can't go into the basement anymore. There's nothing down there but patterns, besides.

And the postman visits, which is hardly a visit at all. He's only supposed to drop the mail through the slot and be on his way. But the postman is a bad man who has been thinking bad thoughts about Mother for a very long time. Ever since he glanced her from the street through the attic window while she was working, he's always wondered if she lives alone and how easy it might be to slip inside one afternoon to do bad things to Mother.

How easy indeed. Unlike Mother's illness, the postman's brain problems work in reverse. As Mother's thought patterns fade, the postman's only intensify. Soon, where Mother thinks of nothing, she is all that he can think about.

And with intensity comes action. He does find a key to the front door. It's sitting there in the rock garden free for anybody to use. He brings latex gloves with him all week after finding the key — gathering up his nerves to actually go inside. And then one day he makes up his mind for real and lets himself in.

The walls are black — the real patterns of the house bleed through the wallpaper patterns that are there to make everybody who visits more comfortable. To the postman, it just looks like mold, of course. He pays it no mind. And it is just mold. But it is also something else too. And this is what the postman won't be expecting.

Then it's about the patterns, less the mold. And that's all Mother can really grasp these days. DNA has a pattern too — and this is what the black stuff growing out of the basement is based upon. It stretched up out of the basement and reached the attic where Mother toils a long while ago. And it overtook some of her dolls too — creeping along their artificial skin surfaces and eventually seeping inside of them.

Patterns. Inside the dolls, it grows in new patterns. Inside, the patterns of the human body form as black knots that quietly become liver, heart, lungs, esophagus. It eats away at the artificial insides to make room for its fetid living growth. There are as many of them as Mother can make. Her work is slow, but she is old. One day she will drop dead and leave them behind. If she still had her mind, she might like to think they would carry her downstairs and bury her in the basement with the others. Thankfully, she can no longer think about the basement, so everything is all right.

He climbs the stairs towards the attic. He takes them two at a time — which is a pattern of his. He's met at the top of the stairs by both darkness and the sound of hard feet on soft carpet. He doesn't know what it means so he just stands there. When their painted white faces emerge through the blackness, he understands too late that this was a bad idea. Not even a bad man idea, just a bad idea.

Then he's falling backward down the stairs. Then he's being carried away. They put him in the basement where it's dark and quiet. Dark and quiet like their home inside the walls. Dark and quiet like Mother happens to be. These are patterns too. They no longer learn or progress. They can't. So they can only protect their matron and put him somewhere safe and make sure that he never gets back up near the attic again.

When he is down there, it quickly moves over him like a mass of black fishing netting and very soon afterward, he becomes part of the spiral that corkscrews up from the basement to spread and permeate throughout the entire household.

Still Mother continues to build, mindless but for the patterns in her head, and still it continues to inhabit, also mindless — except for the patterns that it owns.

There's something wrong with the house.

It starts with the wallpaper and ends in patterns.

There's something wrong with the house.

* * *

Jeffery is twelve. Just trying to play baseball but Sue Ann can't hit the ball for shit because girls never can. So they trade and very quickly they discover Sue Ann can't throw for shit either. He's hit the ball out of the backyard on her second throw, and while that's funny to see her crying again, he has to go get the ball back, and it's in the garden of the Night House.

The Night House. It's what he calls the big place right behind his home. He's been watching the old lady working through the night from the top bunk in his bedroom. When he should be asleep, he's not. He's up watching her — postman in training maybe. Maybe not.

The Night House from a comic book — a witch lives inside and eats children. He can see others in the attic window too sometimes. Robots. And they eat children too. Skin them and then use their baby fat for fuel. Skin off their faces and put them overtop their steel faces to wear like masks. Only teenagers are safe, and Jeffery isn't a teenager. Is he?

He hops the fence. Sue Ann doesn't want to be left alone, and she wants to come as well. He lets her. Looks up her dress while she's climbing over the fence. Then the children push into the tangle of the backyard to find their lost baseball.

They find it, but nobody wants to touch it. It's snug against the bricks at the corner of the house. And it has turned black. Like a little sphere of onyx crafted solely to scare children. Sue Ann starts crying again, but Jeffrey doesn't find it funny anymore. Nothing is funny suddenly.

All of a sudden, all he can think about is how the baseball that used to make Sue Ann cry has become something else that's making Sue Ann cry.

Then there's a robot coming out of the house and making its way towards them. It's broad daylight, and it isn't supposed to be doing that. Maybe Sue Ann's crying disturbed it. He doesn't know, but he runs for it. He leaves her behind for the robot to skin her to pieces and wear her like a new pair of pants. He changes his mind halfway across the backyard. He turns to go back. It's got her, and it's almost inside the house. Far enough away that he can grab the baseball. He grabs it and uses his shirt to pick it up just in case. Gets back to the house and runs inside.

There are patterns here. And they're already forming again.

It's a problem in Jeffrey's plan. Now Sue Ann is missing, but he also has the black sphere from the Night House in his possession, and they might find it. Anyone could find it.

So what to do? Hide it somewhere in the dark and quiet. Hide it in his room, in the bottom of his clothing cabinet where he keeps his socks. Of course, at night in his sleep, it comes to him in a dream that the sphere should not be hidden in such an obvious place.

Like a much-practiced somnambulist, he rises out of bed to take the sphere from the drawer and carry it past the main floor all the way down to the basement. He hides it behind the boiler where it is darker and quieter than before. Then he's awake, and he pisses his pajama pants.

He's standing there wondering how he got into the basement and trying to wipe the black gunk off his palms. No recollection of the black sphere, playing baseball, or Sue Ann.

Patterns get into your brain. Like the way that you swing a baseball bat, or the dozen or so ways you know to make your little sister cry, or when you piss your pants at a specific time in early morning every day because the robots from the Night House are coming to get you. This time it's that black pattern from behind the wallpaper growing upwards from the place in the basement where you buried your dead family members.

New blueprints that get into your brain while you sleep like a cloud of spores. They add new architecture to the things that already exist inside of there. Add new thoughts and new dreams that are alien to everything else you thought that you knew. Eventually, there's nothing left but the pattern — everything else is indistinguishable and no longer matters.

Jeffrey makes his way out of the basement. Back up the stairs to the second floor landing and into his bedroom and eventually, his bed. He sleeps. The whole family sleeps. They sleep as the new thing in the basement quietly basks in the warm heat from the side of the boiler. Then it spreads and spreads.

It yawns out and upward through the walls beneath the wallpaper.

They don't wake again. They only dream of these new things — a new existence in the void.

* * *

Things spiral outwards.

The three of them come dressed in armor. Not government because such things hardly exist anymore. Something different and rag-tag and pieced together from the tattered remains of things that existed before the pattern came and bled through the fabric of reality.

Their suits are etched and pitted with scars from where the acid from its blooms has eaten away at the steel. Blackened patches also scar them. Not from growth but from the scorching blasts of their own flamethrowers.

The suits used to be impenetrable, but age and time and lack of resources to repair does make the armor weaker. The pattern can get in if left to crawl and seek a way to seep through the gaps. They lost Eric first. His face vanished behind his faceplate as the rot set in and replaced it with a visage of blackness. Then they had to kill him a second time. It is hard to destroy a fireproof suit when all you have at hand is fire — but they managed.

It feels as if it has taken forever to fight their way to the place where Mother waits. But they are finally here.

In the passing time, the house has continued to grow upward. A huge column of black and knotty tissue spirals up infinitely into the sky. It is so high that its apex can no longer be seen. Even in the grey daylight.

Things grow in it too. Beyond the acid-spewing blooms that seem so commonplace these days, it has grown what seems a collection of writhing and misshapen limbs that grasp into the air always seeking new prey to absorb.

Somewhere in the center of it sits Mother. Not quite dead but not quite alive either — plugged in, as she is.

Others have been here before. It is the only way the group knows this. Others have not survived to tell the tale but for a few sporadic clues between the bursts of static in their two-way radios. A pale figure at the center of the column's mass.

[We going in, Hailey?]

The question is asked through her headset and emphasized with a blast of piercing feedback at the end of it. Don blasts the ground in front of them with his flamethrower to drive home his point that he's anxious to get to work. He wants to burn through the mass to kill Mother. And he wants to do it yesterday.

But she's tired. Maybe the brain fatigue is getting to her, but they've fought long and hard to get to this point, and there is no turning back as badly as she just wants to do that.

After all, what exactly are they saving? At some point, it was feasible. But things have grown so far and so fast that she's not sure that there's anything left but the blackness.

[No.]

They both respond simultaneously, questioning her

decision. The dual wavelengths result in a massive burst of static that causes a pain so great she almost tears off her helmet and throws it to the ground. She doesn't, of course. That would lead to death - or assimilation.

Once she's recovered, she responds.

[I have a better idea.]

She begins to climb, and they follow her lead. They burn only those limbs that grasp close enough to tear them from the column and drop them to their deaths.

Perhaps they are not here to kill Mother after all. Perhaps the pattern does exist for a reason: to feed the pillar and enable it to grow ever higher. What lies at its apex, though? Maybe they are destined to discover it.

Valhalla? Heaven? Paradise? There are always discrepancies even in the most thought out of formulae.

Frost begins to form on the steel of their armor when she decides ultimately... that ascending is the only variable that she can discern in an otherwise impenetrable and infinite pattern.

Candy Lady

by
Neil Davies

Dennis Wells watched the Candy Lady walk the wet sand of Point Clear.

It took him several long, frustrating seconds to get the focus on the binoculars just right. For a moment he was worried he had lost her, but she wasn't difficult to find again, her bright pink skirt a beacon at the water's edge. As he watched her, following her every move in magnified close-up, he knew he had a problem. She was becoming more than just an anonymous victim, more than just the bait in another of his many traps. She was becoming a *person,* and he was falling in love with her. His Candy Lady.

She had arrived in the Stalking Ground just two days ago, alone and with nothing but her handbag and a small overnight case. From where he sat, outside the Coach House Café at Brightlingsea harbour watching the raspberry sorbet ice cream in his hand slowly melting in the sun, she was impossible to ignore. The pink skirt, tight round the hips, gently flaring out to flap around her legs just below the knee, the same skirt that made her so easy to spot through the dubious focus of the binoculars, brought life and colour to the otherwise grey and faintly shabby surroundings of the typical Essex town. The pink skirt, the pink ice cream, memories of brightly coloured sweet jars... he named her Candy Lady there and then.

He was distracted by shuffling at a nearby table and watched a man in his early thirties lean forward, the delicate, almost feminine contours of his face anachronistic above the gym and steroid developed muscles displayed by the sleeveless t-shirt he wore. The face remained impassive, but the body language was clear. Grant Heddison, Dennis's reason for being in the South of England, had also seen Candy Lady and was equally captivated by her. That should be good, it meant everything was in place, and the plan could progress. Nevertheless, his stomach knotted uncharacteristically, and he felt a fluttering of uncertainty.

The Candy Lady, oblivious to the attention of the two men nearby, moved off at a stroll towards the far side of the harbour. Dennis followed. He did not look back at Heddison, understanding the man's pattern well enough to know there was no immediate threat and he was safe to concentrate on the woman ahead of him.

She was perfect. Not too tall, just over five foot, not too skinny, blonde, late twenties to early thirties. If he had designed the perfect bait for his trap, it would have looked just like her. In truth, he *had* designed it, on paper, scanned into the computer, digitised, 3D, lifelike... but even he hadn't thought of the almost fluorescent pink skirt, the bright blue top. She was *more* than perfect. The unfamiliar knot in his stomach was so tight he felt physically sick.

She walked up the steps and into the concrete complex of stylish apartments overlooking the marina. He watched her enter one of the buildings, dropped the remains of his uneaten, melted ice cream cone into a nearby bin, wiped his sticky hand on his jeans and walked into the nearby public toilets where he locked himself into a cubicle and masturbated. She really was *that* perfect.

Over on Point Clear a family had drifted close to where his Candy Lady stood watching the grey North Sea advancing slowly over sand still wet from the last high tide. For a moment, the daughter of the family pulled his attention away with her long legs, denim shorts and far too tight t-shirt, but she was too young, probably still in her teens, and brunette. She was not perfect enough to persuade Heddison to change his target. Even so, the family group was getting too close and could interfere, and there was a part of his mind that wished they would. For the first time that day, he began to sweat.

The day after her arrival, he had waited, drinking tea at Triscini's wine and coffee bar on the edge of the residential site, until she pushed her way through the double doors of her apartment block. Her choice of clothing was slightly disappointing, black leggings and a green t-shirt, but everything else about her was just as he remembered, just as he had dreamed about in the night.

He was thankful that Grant Heddison, true to his form, had stayed away to prepare. He suppressed a pang of guilt. He should have been watching Heddison, not the woman, but he was confused and driven by his need to see her again. It went against his professional judgement. He was helpless before these strange feelings and compulsions.

Once again, it was easy to follow as she spent an hour or so around the harbour, treating herself to a cone of chips from the Waterside Café, sitting on a bench in front of the yacht club to eat them while watching small pleasure boats drift back and forth on the placid water. After throwing the empty paper cone into a bin, she headed for the bus stop, and he stopped following. The boundaries of the Stalking Ground were very strict, and she was about to travel beyond them. He dare not stray too far from Heddison.

It was easy to scoop the paper cone out of the waste bin, and he once again utilised the cubicle in the public toilets. This time, masturbating into the paper cone her fingers had plucked chips from added an extra *frisson* that made his orgasm even stronger. Afterwards he felt exhausted, drained and confused. Could he abandon his months of planning, his careful trailing of the volatile Grant Heddison, all for a woman he barely knew?

The third day, today, he had once again waited alone at Triscini's. This time his Candy Lady did not disappoint.

She was wearing the same pink skirt as on the first day but with a different, purple, t-shirt. He was excited, nervous, his knotted stomach twisting harder than ever as she made to walk towards the harbour and then changed her mind, heading for the wine bar where he sat.

She took a table one over from his and smiled as the waitress took her order for black coffee. He fought hard not to stare while also struggling with the compulsion to run. She was too close. He felt the blood rushing to his cheeks.

"Excuse me?"

For a moment, he did not react to the soft voice. He sat frozen in his seat, hoping she was talking to a returning waitress.

"Sorry to interrupt you but I wondered if you knew the times of the ferry to Point Clear?"

A short, frantic turn of the head confirmed the worst. There was no one else. She was talking to him.

He felt sick, and his voice broke as he tried to reply. He coughed, forced a smile. How could she affect him this way? He tried to speak again.

"I think they run about every fifteen minutes or so. I'm only visiting so I'm not too sure. Sorry."

She returned his smile, and the knot in his stomach unraveled and twisted again tighter than ever.

"Sorry, I thought you lived round here."

"No problem." Why was he still talking? She had ended the conversation. He had a perfect escape route, and yet he could not stop himself. "I'm a collector, down here on business."

To his surprise, she showed a genuine interest.

"Anything rare?"

"Probably not, although some earlier pieces from the collection did make it into the national papers."

"Really? I only work in an office. I wish I had an interesting job like yours."

He smiled but said nothing more as she finished her coffee, left the money on the table, and rose from her seat.

"Well, thank you for your help..." She raised an inquisitive eyebrow.

"Dennis," he said, quickly, immediately cursing himself for using his real name.

"Dennis." She smiled. "I'm Andrea. I'd love to chat a bit longer, but I've promised myself I'd get over to Point Clear early today. Maybe we could meet later?"

"Yes, I'd like that." And to his surprise he found he would, although he knew it was not likely to be under pleasant circumstances. He felt sad about that, disappointed, and that scared him more than anything else.

He watched her walk away, turning her head once to smile back at him. As he returned the smile, he saw Heddison, leaning against the nearby railings, looking out over the moored boats but only truly seeing the Candy Lady. His hand trembled as he signaled for the waitress to bring his bill. He had told the truth, he *was* a collector, but was he willing to pay the full price this time?

He paid for his tea and was not surprised, when he looked up again, to see that Heddison had gone, no doubt having overheard the short conversation. He would be heading for his van. Dennis took a deep breath to steady himself and, picking up the binoculars' case from by his feet, walked unhurriedly to the nearest semi-circular viewing platform built as part of the new apartment complex. He simply needed to treat this like any other business deal and not get personally involved. He had already risked too much by changing his plans.

He pulled the binoculars from their case and stood at the railings, the marina spreading before him and, directly opposite, Point Clear, barely rising out of the water, empty sand and sparse grass, a café and amusement arcade out of sight over the slight swell of the land. Behind, apartment balconies overlooked him, but he ignored them. He was just another tourist enjoying the view. Nothing suspicious.

He turned first towards the floating quayside to his left, finding his Candy Lady stepping carefully past the parents and children crab fishing off the edge. He could see the top of the small flat-bottomed boat that was the foot ferry, but there were too many people for him to see her actually board the boat. For a short while, he scanned back and forth, worried she might change her mind, but after five minutes, when the ferry left the quayside, his Candy Lady was the only passenger.

He relaxed a little as the family moved away, heading back towards the café and amusements, leaving Candy Lady alone once more on the sand. And now came the silver van with perfect timing, driving slowly down onto the sand, the family stepping to one side to let it through. It was not uncommon. Cars often parked near the water's edge, their occupants looking out to sea, not caring to step outside and brave the typically changeable British weather. No one would pay much attention to a silver van being driven slowly and carefully on the sands of Point Clear. No one but him. But then, he'd been waiting for this.

He was shifting his weight nervously from foot to foot, but it was not possible to stay still while watching the drama unfold. He knew what was coming, had witnessed similar scenes many times before, but for the first time, he fought the feeling that he should do something, be there, protect his Candy Lady.

Andrea. He was unsure whether he had ever known the name of a victim, at least before the event. Once it made the papers he would see the name, read about the family, but it never felt important. It never made them any more *real!* *Andrea.* It was uncomfortable, unsettling. He struggled to hold the binoculars steady, his hands trembling, his stomach convulsing, cramping. He did not know what to do. It was an unfamiliar and unwelcome feeling.

The silver van crept closer to her as she walked, unaware, along the water's edge. He concentrated on the technique, striving to be clinical, professional, as the van stopped and Heddison, with adrenalin-fuelled speed, leapt from the driver's seat.

She struggled. Her legs kicked out from under the pink skirt, she clawed at the large arm around her throat. Through the binoculars, he was able to see the whole thing up close, see the fear, the panic in her eyes, and the ease with which Heddison threw her into the back of the van. It was as smooth and professional an abduction as he had ever seen, but he felt light-headed and nauseous. The impressive demonstration of technique did not, for once, bring forth admiration for the perpetrator but anger and hatred and fear for the victim.

He had to do something. He could not allow this to continue to its natural and, before now, desired conclusion. It risked everything he had planned for, but he could not leave his Candy Lady, Andrea, to her fate. The thought made him sick.

He hurried, pushing the binoculars into their case as he ran back towards the harbour and his car. Heddison worked fast. He could not afford to delay.

The engine started first time, despite the shake in his hand as he turned the key. He crashed the gears finding first, began to pull away from the kerb and slammed his foot on the brake. A tractor. A *fucking tractor* towing a small boat down towards the receding tide, blocking him in as it manoeuvred its way through the narrow street.

He slammed the steering wheel in frustration, the unfamiliar sting of tears in his eyes. Everything was wrong about this, everything was strange and unsettling and *wrong*! He was a professional. He had never experienced any difficulties before, and he had pursued many like Heddison in his life. But he had never seen a victim like the Candy Lady before, *his* Candy Lady, his Andrea.

He refused to dwell on thoughts of where Heddison might be right now, how far along his set, almost religious ritual he would have proceeded, how much fear and panic and agony Andrea might be experiencing. He could not bear to think of that.

With deliberate and cruel slowness, the tractor pulled its load between the parked cars and curious bystanders while Dennis edged his car inch by inch towards freedom. The moment he felt the gap was wide enough, he pushed the accelerator and twisted the wheel catching the bow of the towed boat a glancing blow, cracking the glass of his headlight and showering splinters from the damaged hull, bringing cries of surprise and some anger from those standing nearby. He did not care, even if anyone noted the registration number of his car, he did not care. Once this was over, he would dump the car, and the false identity he had hired it under was untraceable. He was no amateur.

He ignored the speed limits, powering the deliberately unremarkable Ford Focus round tight bends and between parked cars, dismissing all rules of right-of-way, bringing angry beeps and shouts from other motorists. It was a risk he had to take, hoping that the lack of police cars he had noted during his short stay would continue for a little while longer.

Heddison had fewer miles to travel but would be carefully obeying all the rules of the road, not taking any chances. Dennis smiled grimly. He *had* to take those chances.

He pulled on the wheel, swerving. He narrowly missed a car edging too far out of its driveway, swearing over his shoulder as he pushed the accelerator to the floor.

Heddison was illegally squatting in an old abandoned storage shed, off the main roads and protected from view by high hedges. Dennis had located it on his first day in the area. After his research into Heddison, his methods, his personal collecting obsession, it had been easy. Once you understood the man, the rest fell into place.

Following the old local signs for Clacton, he sped through Thorrington, alternating brake and accelerator round the narrow winding lanes, finally turning down towards St Osyth. Almost there.

Had he not scouted the area previously, he would have missed it. Other than a dirt track, barely wide enough for one car, breaking the otherwise verdant roadside there was no sign of the building he knew to be in the field behind the hedges, and no sign of Heddison's van.

He swung into the gap, his back wheels spinning on the dirt, unworried about alerting Heddison to his presence. Even allowing for heavy traffic, Heddison would have arrived at least ten minutes ago and would by now be oblivious to almost anything except his victim. The original plan no longer applied. Stealth and subtlety were not an option if he wanted to interrupt Heddison with his Candy Lady.

In a cloud of dust, he skidded the car to a stop near a weathered clapboard building, flayed skin of pale green paint peeling from the wood, lying scab-like on the well-trod ground. Weeds, running wild through neglect, insinuated themselves between the planks and forced them outwards, giving the wall a bloated, pregnant look. Window shutters hung from broken hinges, and rusted, corrugated iron sheets slipped over the edges of the roof. And yet, it was not possible to see inside the building as all gaps, holes and windows had been painstakingly covered from the inside. This illegal squatter needed privacy to work.

Hurrying from his car, Dennis found Heddison's silver van parked round the back near the door. He hesitated. The heavy wood of the door was as old as everything else, but the hinges and lock were new and sturdy. He would not be able to break it down. This close he could hear faint sounds from within, his Candy Lady, Andrea, pleading, begging, her voice growing weaker as he listened. Despite his rising panic, he had no choice. He had to pick the lock.

It was a difficult one to crack, took him almost thirty seconds, but he knew he'd get it. He was good at what he did.

He pushed through the unlocked door, through a small room that may once have been an office, and into the open storage area where Heddison stood in the glow of candlelight and a single 60 watt bulb hanging from a frayed cord. Normally Dennis would have admired the sight, and, even in his current agitated state, he could not completely suppress his aesthetic appreciation of the ambience Heddison had created. But the reality of how much the delay of the tractor at the harbour had cost him, hit him in the stomach like a heavy fist. He gasped, feeling nauseous, light-headed once more.

The Candy Lady's pink skirt, the one that had first caught his attention, was pinned to the side wall by two six inch nails. It had been tastefully sliced in a zigzag pattern, and a strip of flayed skin trailed delicately from the hem. It was a beautiful touch, and one he would, at any other time and with any other victim, have appreciated. The purple t-shirt hung next to it gripped by pale, delicate fingers. Five nails formed a star shape where they had been driven through the back of the hand and into the wall. Blood still dripped from the severed wrist trailing an abstract pattern of dots and dashes down the wall to the floor. Heddison had already taken his trophy, another for his growing collection, and Dennis's heart seemed to stop for a moment, causing him to clutch at his chest.

The girl herself, Andrea, his Candy Lady, minus a hand and a long strip of skin from her leg, was tied naked and spread-eagled backwards over a large wooden barrel. She was alive, despite the loss of blood from her severed hand, but her position, her open-legged nakedness and the semen spotting her inner thighs were heartbreaking evidence of his failure.

She had seen him, was pleading with her eyes, tearful and dull as she fought to hold onto life. He forced a smile, knowing as he did that this unfamiliar and unwelcome emotion, this *love* that had bludgeoned its way into his heart, his head, was of little use now other than as a source of heavy, deep pain. He could not save his Candy Lady, but he could salvage his original purpose in travelling to

Heddison's Stalking Ground. Was that callous? A stubborn voice told him *yes,* but his professionalism and longtime devotion to the collection said *no*, just common sense.

Heddison himself had been slow to sense the other's presence. Indeed Dennis thought it was probably his Candy Lady and her pleading moan in his direction that first made the killer turn and notice him.

Naked and aroused, with a bloodied hacksaw in one hand and an equally bloodied hammer in the other, Heddison roared in surprise and anger and ran at him.

Dennis, on more familiar ground, was disappointed. He had expected better.

He sidestepped the clumsy swing of the hammer, pulling his favoured nine-inch serrated dagger from its sheath nestling beneath his shirt at the base of his spine, and plunged it deep into Heddison's six-pack. The wet sound of metal sliding into flesh and muscle sent a thrill of excitement through him and he twisted the blade before withdrawing it with an even louder and more satisfying *slop*. Bits of Heddison fell to the floor in gobbets of blood and gore from the hole the dagger had made. The pattern was random but effective.

With a minimum of movement, Dennis drew the blade across the back of the other man's leg, severing the hamstring. As that leg crumbled beneath the naked man and he began to fall, Dennis stabbed lightly, with small penetration only, into the kidneys. The pain inflicted was excruciating, as evidenced by Heddison's surprisingly high-pitched scream, but the damage not enough to kill.

Dennis nudged the falling man, turning him so he landed on his back, and removed the hammer and hacksaw from him with no resistance. Heddison glared at him through his agony.

Glancing back to his wide-eyed Candy Lady, struggling to watch the action, he smiled at her once more, but already he could feel the emotion draining, withering, beaten down by the overriding compulsion that had led him to his chosen profession.

He used the hacksaw to remove Heddison's right hand, in a tribute to the killer's own collection, and taking hold of his still erect penis, which was quite impressive in itself, sawed at the root until it pulled free. For a moment, as the mutilated man screamed and writhed on the floor beneath him, Dennis stopped and admired the spurts and pooling of blood forming a piece of modern art that, he felt, would not be out of place in the Tate Gallery.

Aware that death was fast overtaking the man on the floor he took his knife once more and gouged out the eyes with a sharp twisting of the blade to ensure nice, round bloody holes. He used Heddison's own hammer to knock out the teeth and, finally, the hacksaw to separate the head from the body. He liked to use a fellow collector's own tools wherever possible. He considered it only decent and fair.

His Candy Lady, weak from blood loss, stared at him, frightened but relieved it was all over. He smiled and walked to her.

"Hello Andrea. I'm sorry I wasn't quicker. I tried." To his surprise, there were tears in his eyes and he wiped them away, staring at his damp hand in wonder. This was all so strange. He leant closer to the still bound form of his Candy Lady, whispered, "I love you," and knew it was true. For the first time in his life, he had experienced love, something he had not felt even for his mother back before she abandoned him. It was powerful, almost overwhelming, but ultimately useless and, as thrills go, could not compare to collecting.

He pulled his blade across her exposed throat.

The shock and surprise in her eyes was pleasing, as were the ribbons of blood from the gash in her neck, but it was not true pleasure, just a necessity he found vaguely saddening. She was not the one he had come for.

Kneeling on the floor, holding the severed head of the serial killer firmly between his thighs, he sewed the toothless mouth closed using a surgical needle and thread from the sewing kit he always carried on his belt, small, neat stitches sealing the lips in a karmic smile. Early in his career, he had sewed the eyelids closed too, but as his collection progressed, he preferred to admire the bloodied eye sockets in their open, sightless gaze.

He lifted the head in admiration. A fine addition.

While it might be true that the serial killers, like Heddison, who collected trophies of their victims were serious collectors, he was the one and only *supreme* collector.

He collected the collectors.

Armoire

by
Louise Bohmer

"He's behind me right now, isn't he?" Xian leaned forward, tented his fingers over a book bound in leather, and studied her with eyes so brown they were almost black. "Your expression tells a story."

Ophelia felt her face tense in a mask of fear. The shadow man stepped away from the single bulb covered by a green light shade, which dangled just above Xian.

She nodded, watching the shadow man stroke a wispy hand over Xian's shoulder, before the illusion wedged himself in a slender space between two filing cabinets.

"I felt him then." Blue smoke drifted up, forming a halo around her mentor's slicked back hair. "He's been in there a while." Rising from his plush, leather office chair, he tapped Ophelia's forehead. "You're still collecting rather than banishing, aren't you?" He blew three rings, watched them float away, then pinned her with another cold, matter-of-fact stare.

"But if I see them," she whispered, "I feel safe. In the jars, they can't hurt me."

The man sitting across from her was the real deal. Not just a tarot reader looking for a quick fifty bucks. Mother told her he was born in Vietnam. Spent a great deal of time studying shamanism as he made his way through India, the Middle East, Europe, and eventually here, to North America, where he'd studied with her mother, until she died from a brain aneurysm. When he gave her occult advice, she trusted it implicitly. In esoteric circles she once frequented, rumor had it he was her father, but he'd neither confirmed nor denied it.

"And what has this one done?" After crushing out his cigarette, he threw his hands up in the air. "This isn't the first time one has gotten loose and embedded in your brain. You should be banishing the parasites, not binding them to this world. An extended stay only allows them more power over you. You know that. Not to mention, you've trapped their brothers and sisters, mothers and fathers, in there. It's inevitable they'll come seeking revenge."

She fidgeted with the hem of her sweater, looked away from his gaze that saw all within her. "They're getting trickier. I lock the armoire every night. They're still getting out."

He sighed and rubbed his brow as he frowned. "And why do you suppose that is? Your lessons are sorely behind. Would it kill you to come to me once a week for our sessions? It's been over a year. This isn't like riding a bike, you know? Training is constant, and diligence is a must."

Nodding, she huffed her red bangs out of her face. Now, would he throw the whole, 'your mother would be so disappointed you're not following in her footsteps,' spiel at her? She hoped not. Instead, he took a different track, but no relief came. His next question clenched a cold, tight fist around her stomach.

"Does Marta know about the inter-dimensional parasites you're keeping in your mother's armoire?" Xian's eyebrow rose.

Ophelia watched the shadow man while he swung the lamp behind Xian. The illusion pinned her with those eyes, and she could not tear her focus away. They were brilliant blue almonds with only a pupil. No whites, and no other features on the man's smoky face — if it could be called a face at all.

"Look away from him." Xian broke through her terror trance. "Look at me. Does Marta know?"

Ignoring the shadow man, she shook her head. "She knows the armoire belonged to my mom, but I don't tell her a lot about life … before. She knows you. That's about all."

"Well, she's in for a nasty surprise then." He scanned the day planner splayed open before him. "I've got a non-denominational exorcism in twenty minutes. It's the Catholic priest's first time, and I don't want to leave him alone with that grumpy Celtic shaman I've got coming in. Can we do the purging this evening? "

"That'll be fine," Ophelia said, watching her murky tormentor float to the front of the desk where he perched, crossing one wispy trouser leg over another. His stare always glowed, cutting through the darkness his fedora cast over his eyes.

She got up to leave, but Xian stopped her with a hand placed on her shoulder before she got to the door.

"Marta will need to be a part of the purging. She's unprotected, so we should teach her some defense tactics, as well. You can't keep inter-dimensional parasites in jars and not expect them to take an interest in your girlfriend."

"Yes." She tried not to worry about Marta's reaction to all this occult intrigue. "I'll go home and sit her down. Tell her everything I can before you arrive."

He gave her a soft smile then, and a quick hug. "I'll be there in less than four hours. I promise."

The shadow man flicked a forked tongue over Xian's ear, wagging this sludgy root at her from between squirming lips. If the occultist noticed the shadow man's nearness, he didn't show it this time.

"You will not eat my fear for supper," she whispered to the illusion as she tapped her forehead. "Not today."

* * *

"We need to talk," Ophelia told Marta, as she helped her partner put the last of the groceries away. Ophelia arrived home at the same time as Marta, only to find her balancing an armful of cloth bags.

"What's up, sweetie?" Marta tucked a bottle of milk in the fridge and then turned to her.

Ophelia led her from the kitchen. "You know the armoire in the basement...the one mom left me?"

Marta nodded, casting a confused look at the door that led to the lower level of their small house.

Now, as she stood before it, Ophelia's fingers hesitated on the knob. "I'd like to show you what's inside."

She took Marta's hand and led her down the steep, cement stairs leading into the basement. Marta grabbed the light at the top, and soon the pale blue, cement walls clashed with a flood of fluorescent light.

In the very back of the large workshop / storage area, the armoire sat with unpacked boxes crammed up against either side. The polished walnut wardrobe had been in Ophelia's family for at least five generations. It sat on stumpy carved feet that possessed claws, and at its top a carved face poked over, mimicking the appearance of a wood nymph watching from atop a tree. Its two doors were adorned with complex golden locks that ran up the seams. Golden hoop handles rested in the center of each panel.

Ophelia plucked a set of keys from the 'v' of her blouse. With shaking fingers, she removed the silver chain that held the keys. Each one was a struggle to insert into its lock, and her mouth grew drier with every soft click. Ophelia questioned herself, the doubt haunting her like the sinister shadow man. Should she prepare Marta further? What more was there to say?

"My mother was a Siberian shaman." Ophelia licked her lips, stared at the door. "I told you that, right?"

Marta nodded, casting impatient glances between Ophelia and the armoire. "You were supposed to assume full time training this year. Xian says you copped out. I remember."

Ophelia scowled slightly at Marta's choice of words. 'Copped out' cut deep. What did she know about the rigors of esoteric training? Had she been an inter-dimensional parasite beacon since she was four? Ophelia thought not.

"Well, you could say what's in here is a part of my inheritance." Ophelia wrapped her fingers around the hoop handles. "These...creatures zone in on an astral signal I emit. I'm supposed to banish parasites back to their realm when I see them, but I've been collecting them in here instead."

Marta started to look worried. She wrinkled her nose. "Whatever for?"

Ophelia shrugged. Guilt made her drop her gaze from Marta's. "I...I can't seem to help myself. I've grown obsessed with it. But the problem is, I can't contain them very well anymore. They're tricky bastards, and my containment spells are rusty. One got out recently, and..."

Marta laid a hand on her shoulder, so she looked up. Ophelia's eyes were blurred with tears that embarrassed her. Such a fool she'd been. How grateful she was to see a compassionate expression greet her when she met Marta's gaze.

"And?" Marta danced on the verge of fear. Ophelia could see it in her wide, shining eyes.

"And he's in my head."

Marta tried to quickly mask her disgust under a trembling smile, but Ophelia noted it just the same. How could she blame her, though? By rights, Marta should be furious with her. She should be happy with this mild reaction to her secret. But, the worst was yet to come. Ophelia willed the nerves in her stomach to quiet.

"They wrap around your pineal gland. Your third eye." She pointed to her forehead. "They're parasites who broadcast illusion, which they use to mess with you. See, the parasite feeds off the adrenaline rush we experience when we're afraid. They won't kill you, but they can sure scare the shit out of you."

Ophelia thought back to the first parasite that burrowed in her brain. It was her introduction to her innate abilities, and to the shadow man who taunted her those six months before her fifth birthday. He'd grinned out of closets, or pulled her toes when the blankets betrayed them. That parasite had belonged to the same family as the one now coiled tightly around her third eye. They were an ancient kind, and could be difficult to remove. Mother had sought the help of a well-respected sangoma to get rid of that first one.

"The longer they stay in your head, the more influence they have over your environment, and anyone who comes into contact with you. They act like a radio signal that influences all thoughts that come in their range. They can trick you into thinking their glamour is reality."

Marta tapped a toe on the cement, crossed her arms over her chest. "Are you going to open it? I'm not sure I want to see, but I better."

Nodding, Ophelia gripped the loops and concentrated on the door. She spoke the four entrance spells to unbind it, then traced a sigil with a finger to release the final esoteric lock. Before she tugged the loops, she motioned for Marta to come closer.

"Be very careful," she said, as the panels parted. "I can't leave it open for long. They're sneaky beasts."

Nervously, she turned to gauge her girlfriend's reaction. Marta's mouth was frozen half-open, with the rest of her face wrinkled up in a puzzled frown.

Translucent jars filled the six shelves that lined the converted closet. In each one, balls of fiber optic nerves wriggled, pulsing with beads of pinkish light that zipped through their tubular bodies. When they noticed Ophelia and Marta, the parasites showed thin tendrils tipped in barbs shaped like coaxial connectors. They pressed these against the glass of their jars, seeking to feed their hungry clusters.

"I'd better shut this," Ophelia said, when she noticed Marta's glazed eyes. "Xian is coming over this evening to help me — us — deal with this mess."

Before she could swing the doors shut, Marta stopped her. She gave Ophelia a distant but yearning stare. "May I touch one?"

Ophelia swallowed as fear's icy feet tiptoed up her spine. "No. It isn't wise."

Marta's slack-jawed lack of expression curled into an

ugly sneer. "I want to."

Ophelia snapped the panels shut and stood in front of the armoire. "No. They want you to. It's how they get inside. They're like sirens."

As she slipped the first key into its lock, Marta lunged on her back and growled. Ophelia managed to turn it before she threw her off. Marta stumbled and fell to her side on the cement. It gave Ophelia time to secure two more locks before she was on her again.

"You don't know what you're doing." Ophelia grasped her girlfriend's fingers and pried them from her hair.

"Oh, I certainly do," Marta snarled in her ear. "Let me touch one."

Hating herself, Ophelia reared back and clocked Marta a good one on the jaw. The blow staggered her bewitched lover, but it didn't stop her relentless pursuit. She was slower when she lunged this time, though. Ophelia gave her a hard shove that sent her sprawling on the floor once again.

Frantically, she finished locking the armoire, spoke the binding spells and traced the sigil. As she did so, the sealed wardrobe began to jitter violently. Jars banged against its sturdy oak panels, demanding release.

Marta moaned from behind her, and Ophelia turned in time to see her partner stand, rubbing her jaw as she did so.

"I'm sorry, sweetie." She wanted to go to Marta, but was still hesitant to do so. Locking the armoire should've broken the glamour the parasites had cast over her girlfriend, but there were no guarantees, what with Ophelia being so out of practice.

Before Marta could reply, the lights in the basement went out. Cold laughter filled the room. The only illumination spilled in via two small windows to Ophelia's right. In that slice of light, she saw a smear of darkness flit across the room. Then Marta screamed.

The scant light allowed Ophelia to see the stairs, and, luckily, she had left the door open at the top. But she couldn't see Marta in the near complete darkness surrounding her. Before she could step into the gloom to look for her, Marta ran out, gasping, and clutched Ophelia's hand.

"Something touched me." She pinned Ophelia with bulging eyes, childlike in their openness, wet with terror. "Something cold." Rubbing her arm, Marta shivered. "So cold."

The parasite was growing bolder by the moment. Ophelia began to believe this was more than just some random escape and pineal occupation. This was a planned attack. Xian's earlier words wafted through her thoughts: *It's inevitable they'll come seeking revenge.*

"Oh no." Ophelia's gaze locked on the beacon of hope above, spilling through the open door, spotlighting the stairwell. She squeezed Marta's hand. "We need to get upstairs, now."

Marta nodded, and they raced up the cement steps. The breath Ophelia held whooshed out of her as she spotted the kitchen window through the door frame.

Three stairs from the top, Marta's hand fell from hers. Her girlfriend's shriek stole Ophelia's brief calm with a sucker punch of panic. She looked over her shoulder, and the panic upped its assault a notch.

A universe swirled, eating through the sickly-hued paint, breathing in the cement steps beneath. At its center, Marta clutched at stardust. She looked up at Ophelia, and her face became candle wax as it melted into the vortex claiming her.

The vortex spread out, licking oily tongues over the floor and walls, snuffing the sunlight from the tiny basement windows. As the murk below deepened, Ophelia watched arms darker-than-night climb up the front of her armoire. She heard the creak and crack of wood, and she cried out. Before the mass reared up and swallowed her cherished heirloom, she swore it formed a face, which flashed a hideous white smile, then all-encompassing blue eyes winked at her before the wardrobe vanished.

Hugging the doorframe with one arm, Ophelia reached out to Marta, who still fought against the portal's pull. Marta's fingers stretched like taffy, but they found no purchase. Ophelia leaned farther forward, trying not to topple and fall into the hole between worlds.

As quickly as it bloomed, the vortex began to shrink. It would soon take Marta with it. Ophelia shouted words of encouragement, then switched to cursing anything esoteric, as she helplessly watched her lover lose this fight. As the cement stairs reappeared, Marta started to vanish. Frantically, Ophelia chanted spells and scribed sigils over the retreating portal. All her efforts proved futile.

Soon, light crept back through the tiny windows below. To add insult to injury, the basement door swung shut with a bang of finality. Ophelia slapped her forehead hard and cussed her parasite. Then she beat her fists on the cheap wood entrance.

A squeak at the archway leading to the living room. Ophelia's stomach clenched. Her bladder threatened. Still, she turned her head and willed herself to look at black, polished loafers headed her way. Her gaze traveled up the charcoal pants that trailed wisps of smoke. A man in a fedora smiled his toothless, empty smile when she reached his face.

She stood as the shadow man drew nearer. He reached out, taking her chin in his cold fingers — so cold their frosty touch bit her skin. This wasn't her parasite's work, but she knew the touch well. This was his older brother. The same who had tormented her as a child.

"You had, what, six of mine?" he whispered. "Now I have one of yours. You want her back? You need to pay us a visit then. Bring my brother."

He stroked her forehead then walked into her, letting her cells absorb his icy being. The illusion felt all too real. A tingling took over her skin that stole her breath and made her heart beat too fast. In her brain, the parasite wriggled, greedily suckling on her raw panic. Her lungs fought to draw air. Invisible weight crushed her chest.

There were no black, blooming stars. She fainted without realizing it. When she woke up, she was a foot from the glass coffee table. Her cell phone waited there. Thank Ariadne she had Xian on speed dial. Ophelia crawled forward and snatched the small purple phone from the surface. She pushed the button and fell back to the carpet.

"Hello?" Xian sounded rushed. A high pitch howl filtered through the connection, and then she heard someone in the background scream, "Get behind me, Beelzebub!"

"Help," she croaked. "The whole basement went missing. They've taken Marta. And the armoire."

* * *

"Take me to your vortex," Xian said, holding a hand high above his head when Ophelia opened the door.

She crinkled her nose at his mild melodrama. "I've already told you it's in the basement."

He sighed and gave her a scowl. "Humor an old man."

Ophelia led him to the basement door. "It's not there now, but I'm sure you can invoke it."

Xian turned the knob and studied the gloom below. "It's still there. It's just hiding." He opened the black doctor's bag he'd brought along. "Hold this please." Then handed it to Ophelia, withdrawing from it a bottle of nutmeg-colored powder. He uncapped the bottle and blew the contents into the basement, chanted a revealing spell, and carved a sigil in the air.

The vortex started as a point of light, billowing out at breakneck speed to become a swirling cyclone of dark energy. It reared up, kissed the ceiling, and then dropped. Ophelia took deep calming breaths, looked from her mentor to the frenzied portal, and wished she hadn't been so lax with her studies.

"When this is over, we can begin classes again?" Xian looked at her as the walls peeled back to blackness.

"How did you know I was thinking that?"

He chuckled good-naturedly, then took her hand. "Ophelia, our minds were connected before you were born." His mouth set in a grim line of determination. "You ready?"

If she wanted Marta back, she had to go in there. No wimping out. She stared into the glimmering, churning eye of another world. With a deep breath, she nodded to her mentor. "Let's do this then."

On the count of three, they stepped out of their comfortable reality.

* * *

The city stretching before them was dusted in mauve light that reminded Ophelia of Grandmother's old pantsuits. Fat green clouds drifted over the pale purple sky.

She and Xian emerged in a back alley. By the smell of rotten vegetables, Ophelia guessed they were behind a restaurant. With Xian, she crept to the mouth of the alley and peered around the neon-orange wall.

The parasites' world was one of brilliant Technicolor set against a backdrop of grey. It hurt her eyes to look at the neon buildings.

Ahead, the sidewalk was thronged with illusory bodies. In the parasite's world, however, these fleshy facades they projected could carry weight when they needed to. Here, Xian and Ophelia had to be careful. She scanned the parade of sharp teeth, plumage tipped with fierce talons, and heads sporting a multitude of eyes and mouths. In here, the parasites could bite, tear, scratch, simply by plumping up their humanoid flesh suits.

Xian and Ophelia slinked back into the alley. Keeping an eye on the restaurant door, Xian plucked a syringe out of his doctor's bag. He motioned Ophelia closer.

"This will hurt a bit," he whispered, then covered her mouth as he plunged the needle up her nose.

With a muffled cry, Ophelia dropped to her knees. Hot liquid shot up her nostril, burning a trail to her brain. Xian pulled the plunger back. A sickening sucking filled her skull, and she thought grey matter would soon dribble from her nose. He turned the needle on himself and injected the fluid he'd taken from Ophelia, with merely a flinch.

"I've put your parasite to sleep, temporarily. We're going to use his DNA, and this," he pulled free another syringe, this one filled with a cherry-colored cocktail, "to cloak ourselves, and get in that building."

He injected the cherry-colored elixir up his nose, and then hers, following it with the DNA he'd pinched from the parasite, after adding something from a tiny vial. Ophelia's stomach heaved, pressure coiled tight around her head, and her vision blurred as the world tilted sideways.

"Marta's in there?" she slurred, pointing to the fire-engine red, gothic cathedral Xian had indicated.

He nodded. "My spidey sense is tingling."

"You don't have spidey sense."

He frowned at her. "Let's not get stuck on particulars."

After the cloaking serum took effect, they slipped out among the masses, toward the towering cathedral. Ophelia tried not to stare at the parasites dressed in flesh suits. Men with blue tubes sprouting from scalp and nose cavities; women with three orange heads, and six breasts straining their t-shirts; babies with tails like chameleons that turned color when they cried.

The cathedral stood before them. A bloodshot, disapproving eye that dared they enter. Xian kept a nonchalant stance as he pushed the rubbery doors open and beckoned Ophelia follow.

Inside, another surprise greeted them. While the building wore the appearance of a church, the interior was clothed in business management aesthetic from head to toe. Cooing potted plants sat at the end of the hallway. Beyond this, a mass of grey cubicles stretched as far as they could see.

"Other way," Xian said, turning on his heel and walking toward the opposite end of the corridor.

They rounded the corner and found another hallway lined with sturdy, steel doors. Xian touched each one as they passed it. He stopped at one five doors down, flexing his fingers against the metal, and announcing, "Ahah!" After running his fingers down the seam to look for locks, he twisted the knob, which easily turned. "Something's up."

"What?"

He cast a concerned glance her way. "No protection. They want us to come in. That can't be good."

"I had a feeling back in the basement." Ophelia chewed the side of her mouth. "I think we're being set up."

Xian nodded, rubbed his stubbly chin. "Do you remember how to deactivate their glamour when they're not in your head? Marta's definitely not alone in there, and they rarely wrap around your brain when they have you in this world. No need, really."

Thinking back over her training, Ophelia frowned. "I remember bits of the chant, but that's about it." She shook her head in frustration.

Before they opened the door, Xian went over the deactivation procedure with her. He had her repeat the chant twice, and draw him a diagram in the air before they could continue.

Ophelia gave him a glare. "I'm not completely inept, you know."

A creak sounded, as Xian slid the wood away from the jamb. "One can never be too careful."

Inside, Marta sat shackled to an office chair that aspired to be a throne. Intricate scallops adorned the seat, rising high above its back. And standing between these spires was a shadow man. His fingers snaked out from smoky hands, plugging into Marta's orifices. Thumbs squirmed in her ears, index fingers seeped into the corners of her eye sockets, middle fingers wriggled up her nose, ring fingers conspired to stretch her mouth open wide, while the pinkies crawled down her throat.

Ophelia gasped. Marta was grey and sweating. Her limbs jittered as the shadow man milked her terror. Her blue eyes streamed a thick, yellow fluid.

Xian held her back when she made to dash in the room. "Be careful. He has her in a precarious position. We need to negotiate."

"Negotiate?" Ophelia snapped. "Bullshit. He's going to kill her."

Xian nodded. "He could kill her, if he feels threatened."

"Don't talk about me as if I'm not present," the shadow man hissed. "Come in. Your pitiful attempt at cloaking might work with the masses out there, but I can see right through both of you."

As she stepped over the threshold, Ophelia spied movement near a row of towering filing cabinets. A streak of shimmering blue flashed forward, then watery breath came at her ear. As she turned to face this hidden visitor, the shadow man lashed out with a long tendril, attacking Xian, who held up his doctor's bag in defense.

"How's it feel to be trapped, huh?" A fish-headed woman pointed at her with a rainbow fin. "To watch your loved one lay helpless, while you're helpless. You imprisoned my sisters and brothers. You've got my son in your brain."

"He crawled in there. I didn't invite him."

Ophelia remembered what Xian had told her in the hall. She put a lid on her simmering anger and focused her will. *Third tendril lining their torso,* Xian had told her. *It'll stand out on their body. There'll be something unique about it. Grab this and pull with all your might. Speak the words...*

And she did. Fish-head howled through rubbery lips, throwing her head back as she caterwauled and shrank to one third her size. When Ophelia finished the chant, the deactivated parasite floated up from the floor to glare at her with pulsing tubes.

"Here's the deal," Ophelia got in the parasite's non-existent face. "Your son gets out of my head, and his brother gets out of my girlfriend. You stay the hell away from me and Marta for the rest of our lives, and I'll quit collecting. Just straight up banishing and sending your babies back to you from now on. Oh, and I want my armoire back."

"The rest of your lives?" The parasite scoffed. "I can't promise anything there. The children have minds of their own. But, so long as you stick to the rules, I'll do my best. And your armoire will be in your basement, once you cough out my kid."

Ophelia looked over her shoulder to Xian, who had also deactivated the parasite plugged into Marta. Her mentor now propped up her limp girlfriend, while the parasite hovered behind the chair.

Xian stepped in. "Wait a moment. If she spits him out here, you could trap us in this world. Guarantee us safe passage home."

The parasite shivered with visible anger, mimicking a coil of frenzied vipers. "Fine."

Ophelia stepped back as nausea cramped her stomach. Intense pressure built in her head. Her nose filled with water as the parasite detached itself from her pineal and wriggled across her brain, working his way into her mouth. She fell to her knees, a fierce headache slamming her forehead as the parasite, wrapped in a ball of mucous, spread her mouth with his tubular fingers and pulled himself free. He floated to his mother, and the pair cooed to one another softly, while the third drifted over to join them.

"Remember your promise," Xian said, making his way toward Ophelia, but directing the words at the gathering of parasites.

"You know we will," the mother growled. "You'll find a vortex waiting for you in the hallway." She would have to honor the deal. It was a cardinal rule of their world. Bargains with humans were legally and astrally binding. She'd been trumped, and she obviously didn't like it.

A swirling black hole opened in the wall opposite as they

left the office. Before they walked through, Xian stopped Ophelia. "Speaking of promises..."

Irresponsibility had nearly cost her the lady she loved. It was time to overcome this obsession. It was time to swallow her fear of her power.

"I won't forget. No more collecting. And let's resume my training Tuesday evening. How's six o' clock for you?"

Shrieking Gauze

by
Edmund Colell

James adjusts his hospital nametag, and then pulls his gloves on as he approaches the bio-medical waste container. Wearing his dark sunglasses, he looks through the waste he deposited while on duty.

Where's that incision packing from earlier?

He reaches into the container and removes soiled sheets and used nightgowns. Soon he finds needle tips, thermometer covers, and — most importantly — bandages.

Have seven of those, he thinks toward the Band-Aids. *Three,* toward some patches.

Finally, he finds some incision packing pieces. He pulls the first up to his face and stares at it. While staring, he hears a low droning. He stares at another and hears wavering chirps. The colors of blood and pus produce each sound. Everything he sees produces sound. When he was a child, before he had sunglasses, overloads caused him to have seizures.

As he pulls up the third piece of packing, he hears a scream. He jumps back and shuts his eyes, listening for distress outside. Then, as he reopens his eyes to the packing, he hears the scream again. Pulling a plastic bag from his pocket, he lays the packing pieces inside without looking at them again.

His phone vibrates in his pocket. Closing his eyes, he flips it open and says, "Hello?"

"Hey, are you done yet?"

"Yeah, just come around to the back. I'll load the incinerator and see you in a sec, Earl."

* * *

As James crawls into Earl's car, he catches Earl looking at the plastic sticking out of his pocket. "You did it again, didn't you?"

James shrugs his shoulders. "No one's said anything about it."

"You better hope no one does. I'm pretty sure they can fire you for that shit. It's unsanitary."

"I keep everything sanitary in there. They can look the other way if I take a bandage. Isn't it better for a bandage to be in my dorm room than on their floor?"

"I share that dorm with you, too. So what about how I feel?"

James sees the dormitory loom into view among the sunglass-shaded silhouettes of cars and buildings. "You haven't said anything about it before."

Earl snorts. "You're lucky I'm willing to room with just about anyone."

James chuckles. "I hope I'm an interesting roommate at least."

After they pull up, James looks around at the parked cars. He looks for the brightest red paint jobs but hears only whistles or cheers — nothing as loud as the scream of the packing gauze. Similar sounds sing from the red-and-blue colors of their school flag hung in the halls.

* * *

In his room, James opens a chest labeled 'accounting notes.' There are no notes inside. The contents of the chest include bandages and dressings covered with many blood colors in varying states of decay and coagulation. Together, they sound like a low-moaning crowd. He picks through them but still finds no match to today's gauze. He pulls the bag from his pocket and fishes out latex gloves from a box in the chest. He picks up a gray piece of construction paper and a flashlight. Setting these materials on the sink in the bathroom, he shuts the light off and removes his sunglasses.

After holding his eyes closed for a moment, he turns the flashlight on the gray construction paper. Its sound, a soft, static noise, clears his head. His other hand feels around for the bag and picks one of the packing gauzes. He takes a deep breath, preparing to clamp his eyes shut before sliding the packing under the flashlight.

To his relief, the gauze only makes sounds at the pitch of stern speech. Sounds slur between the white gauze, green pus, and brownish-red mix of blood and dirt. He hears vague approvals and groans among them. Despite the incomprehensible gibberish, he leans in to try listening to each component.

Can't believe I haven't tried this before._

As he tires of the stern-sounding piece, he puts it back in the bag and stares at the gray paper again. He breathes deep and fiddles his fingers around the two other pieces in the bag. He settles on one and hesitates as he pulls it into the gray.

His hearing shatters. Tears splash down his face. In the midst of a violent cry, the only word is a focused and piercing 'YOU!'

He clicks the flashlight off and rubs his sore eyes. Between the options of looking at the pure red blood once more or storing it back in the bag, he chooses the latter. With his sunglasses shielding his eyes, he leaves the bathroom. Looking at the hand he used to rub his eyes, the tears he smeared are thick with blood.

James stares at the blood for half a minute feeling heat drain through his ears. Noises pop past his glasses.

When was the last time I bled more than a little?

Thinking of the answer, he returns to his chest. Among the larger bandages, he pulls out a pus-crusted gauze wrap.

As his touch avoids the crusts of scab tissue and dried fluid, he finds a yellow tag with the number one drawn in marker. Out of the entirety of his collection, he still looks at this one the most even though it only croaks few sounds. Laying it back in the chest, he strides over to the medicine cabinet and removes a jar of cotton balls.

Earl walks by with a glass of either water or vodka. He splashes some on his shoes as he double-takes toward the red streaks on James' face. "Jesus Christ," he says, "what happened to your eyes?"

"I think I went overboard," James says. He looks away as he dabs the blood out of his tear ducts and blinks his eyes. "Please, get me a bag."

"You're not seriously going to keep those, are you?"

"Why not?"

"Look, you're bleeding from your eyes because of this. It's not healthy!"

Left with a damp and loaded cotton ball, James steps past Earl to get the bag himself. "It's more than healthy," he says, "it's therapeutic."

Earl sputters taking several steps away. "Did a doctor say you need to look at bandages?"

James shakes his head as he drops the cotton in the bag. He rolls up a sleeve and turns his forearm over. A white scar runs lengthwise from the middle of his arm to his elbow. "It's a lot of blood to watch running out of yourself when you can see blood screaming."

Earl nods but holds his hands out in front of him in defense. "I remember, but that still doesn't explain why you started collecting. I know there was that one guy in high school who started collecting classical albums after he had surgery, because that helped him through it. I mean, did you look at blood and stuff the whole time you were recovering?"

James shakes his head again while he pulls open a drawer and starts fingering through its contents. "Not until the wraps came off. I was too scared before. Blood feels safer to me when it's in a bandage. Maybe bandages could get me over my fear of blood."

"What the hell are you looking for in there?" Earl lays a hand on James' shoulder.

James shuts the drawer. "Do you still have your magnifying glass?" Even as his sunglasses hide his eyes, he feels exposed. He rubs his sticky blood-tear trails and says, "Sorry, you don't need to know about this."

Earl's hand slips off James' shoulder. He starts walking away. "Then leave my magnifying glass alone."

"Wait," James says. "The gauze that made my eyes bleed said something."

A twitching shock passes through Earl's face. "What did it say?"

"A really loud 'you,' like it was accusing me, or commanding me, or something like that. And I heard other things from some other bandages when I took my shades off, but I can't tell what those ones are saying. At least, not without looking closer." Another pause causes James' courage to feel soggy.

"Well," Earl says, "I'll get the magnifying glass and my phone for the hell of it. We'll see if you get anything out of that cotton ball, but I'll be ready in case you get something worse than bleeding eyes."

* * *

With the lights off in their dorm room, James removes his sunglasses and shines the flashlight on the gray paper. His eyes feed on the static gray for a short while, and then he picks up the cotton ball and holds it above the paper. Though softer than the gauze, lively voices chatter among the white and the red. As he reaches for the magnifying glass, he glances up to see Earl standing by with his cell phone in hand.

"Just give me a sec," James says, moving the glass over the paper.

Peering into the magnified grayness, he hears a drone

like the sound of fluorescent lighting. The weight of the droning sound slows him down. Earl and the safety net of his phone keeps James reaching for the cotton. He closes his eyes before sliding the cotton under the glass, and releases a breath while he opens them again.

"Will."

His breathing eases by the time he hears the cotton. Red clumps bellow clear against the scraping white fibers, repeating the word as long as he looks at it. He gives Earl the thumbs-up.

"It says 'will,'" he says. "Together, 'you will' or 'will you.'"

Earl chuckles. "Okay," he says, picking up the rest of James' collection, "let's see where this goes."

An old Band-Aid goes under the magnifying glass. James squints, his hearing muffled by the dark residues of clots and dirt. To the side, as the clot stretches into red streaks, he hears different voices all saying syllables from "Information."

Another Band-Aid says, "More."

A third, "Need."

James stuffs that Band-Aid away and produces a pocket notebook. He slips his sunglasses back on as he holds the flashlight on the notebook and starts writing.

"At least three words connect one way," he says, "but the beginning can still go either way. 'You will' or 'Will you' need more information." As he finishes writing the five words down, he sighs "Either way, no shit."

Earl flips the light switch back on and pockets his phone. "At least it's better than them saying, 'You will burn the school' or something like that. Sometimes first tries suck, but I can't stay up all night to keep watch. Besides, too many in one night will probably blind you. Or deafen you. We can do it tomorrow night if you need to, dude, if it helps you get over this bandage thing."

Left thinking of five words with no conclusion, James taps his finger on the chest and says "Okay. Sorry for keeping you up."

"Seriously, rest your eyes for a while."

* * *

In his room, James sits on the edge of his bed. The shadows and silhouettes give him enough silence to think.

There's no way in hell I'll be able to concentrate in class tomorrow if I can't even sleep. Just a few more and I'll be all right.

Sneaking out of his room, he pads around the living room, blind in the dark. He feels around for the chest and quiets the unlocking with his fingertips. His fingertips work hard to keep the plastic bags from crinkling as he pulls them out. With the bags, flashlight, paper, and magnifying glass on the coffee table, the only stealthy action left is to ease himself onto the couch without squeaking its springs. He sits motionless for five seconds when that fails, but pulls the paper and flashlight towards him once Earl fails to investigate.

Okay.

He refreshes himself with the paper.

Now let's go with another gauze piece.

He shifts his eyes to the side of the magnifying glass before observing the gauze. Slight grumbles from the pus reassure him that this piece is not the 'you' piece. Knowing that, he turns it blood-side-up and puts it under the glass.

"Suffer."

His neck twitches. As with the other words, 'suffer' keeps repeating as long as his eyes remain focused on the blood. He cannot discern any other word, despite wanting it to be more innocent and cohesive, like 'soon.' *You will need more information suffer?*

He switches this gauze for the third one, checking again to make sure it wasn't the loudest piece.

"Pain."

I guess packing gauze is always forceful.

He tries chuckling at the thought but finds that the

chuckles sound more like whimpers. His immediate reaction is to ignore 'need more information' and form 'You will suffer pain.' As that thought lingers, it gels into thoughts about the time his arm was sliced open. That hardens to thoughts about car accidents, burning buildings, wars, and holocausts. His eyes glue to his collection, and for the first time since he began collecting, he doesn't find comfort in them.

No matter how many bandages I keep around, I'll always be a pussy.

Bearing that in mind, he lays another Band-Aid under the glass. It says, "Read." He writes the word down and inserts another one that says, "Wraps." Another says "At." A patch says "To/Too/Two," and a final Band-Aid says "Find."

Why do the Band-Aids and patches have weaker words to say? They all have blood on them, so what makes them different?

He goes through the last two patches: "In" and "The."

After writing all of these words down, James gawks at his jumble of words: "You will need more information suffer pain read wraps at to/too/two find in the."

Is this even meant to give me any kind of message? Is this just a tangle of words that I'm imagining?

He starts writing down the combinations he hasn't tried:

'You need information in pain.'

'You need to read more information.'

'You will suffer in the pain.'

'You will find need at the pain.'

'You will need to read more pain.'

'You will find information in the wraps.'

'Information will suffer.'

'You need to read the wraps.'

From those, he scratches out several until he is left with, 'You will suffer in the pain,' 'You will need to read more pain,' and 'You will find information in the wraps.'

It's still saying that I need more of something, I guess, but it keeps saying something about how something is going to hurt me, too. Not sure if I should drop words or not. And does everything need to start at 'You will?' Is it going to tell me something about the future or is it commanding me to do something?

Flipping to another page in his notebook, he writes, 'You will find information in the wraps' and 'You will need to read more pain.' Outside of 'You' and 'Will,' he checks each of those words off as they appear in his word bank, leaving two words unused. He puts 'You will' before those unused words, and ends up with two sentences and something incomplete:

'You will need to read more pain.'

'You will find information in the wraps.'

'You will suffer at'

The incomplete third statement curdles his stomach as he seeks the answer.

More pain... like how the packing gauze was more forceful than the Band-Aids and patches? It works with the wraps.

A jolt zips through his body, and he turns to the old wraps drooping over the edge of the chest. He grabs it with quaking hands and drags the length under the glass, stretching it across until he magnifies the old and crusted material from before. But as he looks into each crevice and each dry splotch, all he hears are muffled and wheezy vocalizations. Even magnified, he finds no words in long-dead blood. Frustrated sweat breaks out on his forehead, and fearful paralysis sticks him to his seat as the clock drifts into the next day.

Need to complete it. Need to avoid it.

The couch squeaks as he pushes up, and the plastic bags crinkle as he loads them back into the chest, but he makes no effort to quiet them. Earl is tucked away, and no amount of shaking and shouting over an incomplete threat will wake him. James stuffs the magnifying glass into his backpack, trudges back to his bed, and struggles to sleep.

Fuck. Now I can't stop.

* * *

Every joint in James' arms and legs protests as he wakens to his alarm clock. Throughout showering, clothing, eating, and walking to class, he pictures 'You will suffer at.' His eyes ring from the loudness of the sunlight, even behind his sunglasses, but he keeps them open as they follow cars, glance towards construction crews, and shift among other pedestrians. His heart and lungs tighten as he gets close to any of these, and he trots away from each one as soon as possible.

In class, 'You will suffer at' smothers the lecture. James gives more time to watching the clock than to writing notes. When he doesn't watch the clock, he nods off into sleep, only for dreams of ripping flesh to wake him up. By the end of class, a headache prickles his brain.

He nods asleep again outside of a restaurant as he waits for Earl to pick him up for work. The restaurant's cheesy and saucy odors sweeten his unconsciousness against exhaustion and frustration. But as cheese and sauce drift in, they are contaminated by human fat and gore. The restaurant merges with the hospital. James shivers awake when Earl taps him on the shoulder.

* * *

James dumps the scummy tissues from a wastebasket into a bio-medical container. He finds bandages inside but nothing new. Among simple covers and pads, the low-pain values of blood spots whisper to him as he ignores them. He lingers a little longer to try to find wrappings or discarded dressings from trauma patients. Luckless, he lets the lid fall and leaves to return the basket.

On his way, he steps out of the path of a nursing team wheeling a gurney through the hall. His eyes follow the gas tank and the hangar with a nutrient bag to a patient whose head is obscured by yellow-stained wrappings. After his eyes, his body starts to follow the gurney. The gurney and nurses soon disappear behind the door to the burn unit, but James reads the tag on the gurney, Room 473. Before they vanish, he memorizes the number.

"Hey, Jim," a nurse says from behind him, "Ms. Valenzuela needs that basket back."

Panic forces James to turn back around. He chokes his breathing into line as he says, "Right. Sorry, Melissa."

The glance of her eyes from his face to the burn unit grows an embarrassed lump in his stomach, swollen by the querying tones he hears in the colors of her eyes. He nods before taking off, beating himself with Earl's words:

'I'm pretty sure they can fire you for that shit.'

The more he beats himself with those words, the redder his face blushes.

As he rushes back to return the basket, he maps the routes between there and his backpack, between the backpack and Room 473. He connects the burn victim's wraps to the bandage message, but the connection feels loose.

This might not be it, but it's the first shot I have.

His footsteps lengthen to strides, as he dodges around visitors, staff, and patients. Some of them turn to watch, and he avoids their eyes. His eyelids scrunch down to slits as he tries limiting the visual noise, but he splits them open again and again as obstacles force his acknowledgement. He opens the door to Ms. Valenzuela's room, drops the basket inside, then twists back around.

"Are you okay, Jim?" a passing doctor asks.

"Fine, Dr. Rihannon."

"Is there some kind of waste emergency going on that I'm not aware of?" Dr. Rihannon's question fades in the distance as James keeps striding past.

James takes a deep breath on the way to the employee lounge.

A patient in a wheelchair passes him by, his calf covered in wraps discolored red and brown.

"Excuse me, son," says the old man, "could you please refer me to the director's office? I need to make a complaint."

James's throat clenches as he stops to answer.

What if he's the one I'm looking for?

He shoves the thought to the side as he says "Fifth floor, fourth room on the right."

There's no way he would have let me look at his leg, not the way he sounded.

The rest of the way to the employee lounge darkens with thoughts towards the patient in Room 473.

The only way I can get it from him is if he's unconscious, if I want to keep my job.

James stuffs the magnifying glass in his pocket and leaves. His resolve weakens as he presses the call button to the burn unit.

"Where can I find Room 473? I heard the waste baskets need some emptying," he asks the attendant.

"You're welcome to get rid of anything in there. Just get a mask, cap, and gloves from the counter first."

While strapping the mask on and slipping his hands into the gloves, he strides to the door of Room 473. As he greases his gloves with sanitizer from the wall-mounted pump, he peers through the glass. Wrapping his hand around the door handle, he pushes in and eases it shut.

His eyes lock on the patient as he sneaks forward. The sound of the patient's breathing calms him despite carrying smells of fresh leakage from the wounds on his face. James sees a few anguished voices, scattered without magnification, among the wraps. Then, with his eyes closed, he slides his sunglasses off and exchanges them for the magnifying glass. Opening his eyes again, a low cacophony rattles his sight.

I need to be quick.

Random noises blare from every lit surface.

I haven't been this exposed since I was a kid.

He leans down with the magnifying glass and searches the bloodiest strips.

"Freed," one says.

"However," says another.

"Be."

Swallowing, he starts shifting the glass all over the face.

"Be freed however. However be freed."

Blood vessels start breaking in James' eyes from irritation and frustration.

You're shitting me!

"However be freed. However be freed. However be freed."

The chain of "However be freed" ends as he finds a loose strip near the patient's shaved hair.

I'll tell them that it came undone. I just need to know...

James' hand hovers over the loose strip, followed by the magnifying glass. His fingertips grip the end. He draws a deep breath. He pulls.

"NOON!"

James' screams rip louder than the howl of the wound, louder than the howl of the newly-woken patient.

James' eyes gush hot and viscous as he holds them. As he blindly stumbles around, the sickness deepens, worsened by the radiating suffering of the patient. James trips backward over a cord, and his head smashes into the corner of a table. His eyes open once more, and his limbs and digits spasm as the last thing he sees tears the last of the screams from his body.

All is silent. James feels morphine-dulled pains in different bones, different patches of skin, and different muscles. Despite feeling injuries all over, he only feels bandages on his head.

Is all of it real?

Pain runs strongest from his eyes, which feel moist

rather than sticky like his other wounds.

Earl's voice breaks through the silence. "Can he talk?"

James gurgles trying to answer.

"Probably won't speak for a few days." A nurse says. "Dr. Rihannon says his speech will be better than his vision, though. Because his eyes have continued to bleed, he could come out of this blind."

The thing he saw blurs again in James' thoughts.

I don't know if the bandages were a warning or a threat.

He hangs on the latter, as all company leaves the room. He fears that the thing will return while he lies blind and injured.

The patches feel snug against his eyes, and the quiet of the darkness forms a calm void. The wounds, real or imagined, would soon pass into scars. A peaceful smile parts James' lips as he joins the words of the wraps with, "You will."

The Highest and the Sweetest

by
S.P. Miskowski

I started out as one of the babysitters on the day shift. I'm still a babysitter, but I have another career now, too. I'll tell you about my new job in a minute.

I guess I applied about ten times before I got an interview. There's a long line of women that want to do what I'm doing. Women come from all over the country to apply. A few men apply, too, but Quartz only hires women. We've got the natural instinct.

"I feel like this is the work I was born to do."

That's what I told Quartz during the interview. And in a way it's true. I was born to do what I'm doing. You could say it's more of a calling than a job. You could say it's my destiny.

My daddy was sick for a long time before he died. I took care of him night and day. Then when he passed it seemed like all I did was wait for a sign. I kept looking, on every channel. Almost a year passed.

One day when I was packing up some old clothes for the Salvation Army I found a box full of shoes in the back of a closet. One corner of the box had been eaten away. Inside I found a mouse, little brown thing, with six babies. Well, here was a tiny miracle where you would never have expected it.

I cleaned out my sewing basket and then I filled it with some of the clothes I had gathered up for charity. I spent hours finding the warmest spot for the basket, right in the middle of the living room. When everything was just right, I lifted the mouse babies and their mama and put them in their new home.

It must have been a couple of hours later while I was watching "Kate Plus 8" that I heard a sound I'll never forget. Like a squeal, but crazy, with all these scratching noises. That's what I can't get out of my head: the scratching — and chewing.

I jumped up from the couch and pulled back the towel I had draped over my sewing basket. It was the most terrible thing I'd ever seen. That mama mouse had gone insane, somehow, and she was eating those babies! She had killed four already, and the clothes I had used to build her nest were soaked in blood.

I felt like I was choking, like something had hold of my heart and was crushing it. The sight of those tiny naked bodies twitching while their mama, the one who gave them passage into this world, tore their flesh away with her sharp, little teeth! I slammed the remote control down, one time, two times, one last time. Then she stopped moving.

The last two lived another day and a half. I tried every food and every kind of soup. I tried milk and bread. They just lay there, with their hearts beating away and their breathing was fast and shallow. Finally, they died. Their mama didn't give them the love they needed, and they died. It was an awful thing to see, but I learned what I needed to learn.

So the first time I saw Quartz on TV was a revelation and a confirmation, to me. I've prayed all of my life. Every day I've spoken to God and asked what I should do to make my life serve a purpose.

The day I saw Quartz on the TV screen, God reached down and touched me, and I knew why. For the first time, I knew what I was meant to do. I was born to take care of these babies.

The people that write those blogs, those are the monsters. Not Quartz. Not me. Those bloggers are evil.

Can you believe a human being with a soul would say the things they're saying? I don't. My daddy taught me: There are some people who don't have a soul, and they'll take yours if you don't watch out. So I watch out. Nobody's going to take my soul.

Quartz is not a bad mom. That's a crazy thing to say. People who write that should be in jail for trashing her character. She is a beautiful and gracious young woman. Those rumors about her having plastic surgery are lies. She's as natural as the day is long. She could be a model if she wanted to, but she put her life on hold to raise these babies. Most people will never do one thing as beautiful as what Quartz has done.

Here's the part I don't understand: How can the government and the social services tell a woman what she can do with her womb? If you can answer me that, well, okay then. Go ahead.

See? You can't tell Quartz what to do, can you? Not if you're a feminist. And you look like you might be one. If you say she's got the right to do what she wants, then she's got the right to do what she's doing. It cuts both ways, you see, the feminist thing? You can do what you want, and Quartz can do what she wants.

Every one of the babies Quartz is nursing right now is nothing but a gift, a pure gift from Heaven. A baby's soul is the most pure thing you can find in the universe. That's why in certain cults they like to sacrifice the infant, because it's the highest and the sweetest thing. It's a fact of history that some religions have called for strangling the child, or crushing its skull, or even burning the baby alive. There's the proof that children are sacred, right there. Every part of a baby's body is perfect in God's eyes.

The most corrupt thing alive is an evil heart. It's the evil heart in these people that makes them say: "Quartz is a bad mom. Nobody ought to give birth to twelve babies at once, not when she's already got the Octuplets and two sets of Quints."

Or they say: "Who's the father? The fertility clinic?"

Like it's a joke. Let me tell you something, the life of a baby is not a joke. It comes straight to earth from the bosom of God. If you could see Heaven right now, you would see millions and millions of tender, little angels floating in the sky, every one waiting to be born. Every one is waiting for a loving heart to call it to its earthly home. When you deny one of these angels a home in your heart, it's a sin.

Yesterday a man on the radio said: "Why don't they slap that doctor with a lawsuit and put him out of business?"

See? That's hate, right there, nothing but hate. That fertility doctor is serving God's purpose. All he's done is to open a gateway for these babies to come through so that they can serve the Lord.

If you know these things, if you see how it all works, then you're living in the light. If you don't, then I feel sorry for you.

None of those people on TV and the radio shows care what happens to these little angels. They just want to have their way. Well, you know what? They're outnumbered. All the people that send Quartz letters and emails say she's doing something beautiful. Right now we've got several prayer groups that send us a blessing every day.

Now those are righteous people and their concern is righteous. We need those prayers. It took several weeks for the Dozen to open their eyes, and then we knew right off that three of them were blind. Two more went blind later on. You know what? Quartz loves them even more than the ones that can see. That's how she is.

There's one of the Dozen that has to be fed through a tube in its abdomen. Lots of women would be put off by that but not Quartz. She feeds that baby one or more of its meals every day. She fills the plastic bag and hangs it on an IV hook and stands right there, singing a hymn, while the bag drains. She takes over from the nurse whenever the gal needs a break or goes home sick. Quartz jumps right in there like it was nothing. Now you tell me if that's not a good mom.

Just interviewing nurses and babysitters is a full-time job. Quartz handles most of that by herself. She has to be on the phone six hours a day, sometimes. She's got a little office she goes to for that, in a guesthouse she built out back by the pool. It's the only way she can get enough peace and quiet to do what she needs to do. It's hard work. She might go through twenty or thirty babysitters before she finds one like me, with a calling. Not everybody can handle this work.

We had a teenage girl last month, hired part-time to help out. She came in all cheerful and talking about teaching the Quints baby sign language, because she took a class on it. She didn't watch our weekly program on the Angel Babies Network before she started. Some people haven't seen it. Hard to believe, but some people don't watch cable.

So the first time this girl met both sets of the Quints and saw that some of them had the little flippers where the others had fingers and toes, she broke down. We had to get the nurse to give her a sedative. Then the girl's mom came and drove her home, and she never came back. This job's harder than it looks. I'm sure you heard about the one babysitter we had, last year, conned her way in and then tried to poison two of the Octuplets that are on respirators. Said she was on a mission! She was insane. She's locked up now. They ought to throw away the key.

So there are tears, but there's good news, too. Reasons to rejoice. The Octuplets celebrated their fourth birthday last month. You'll see Quartz and the Dozen on a birthday special soon. That was the last thing they taped before the social workers came. The Dozen were all signed up to be in six new episodes next year. That might not happen now. I don't know. You have to ask the lawyers and the producers about it.

The network and donations cover all the legal costs. So there are good people in the world, and you should tune out the people that aren't good. Otherwise, they'll ruin it for everybody.

So many good people love Quartz and the kids. (You all know who you are! You broke the ratings record for the potty training episode with the first set of Quints. We love you, too!) Good people are all over the place. They send cards and presents. They buy clothes and shoes and little custom-made Halloween costumes for the kids.

All Quartz lives for, is the kids. I could literally testify to that, if those social workers would let me. The night Quartz gave birth to the Dozen she nearly died, soaked the sheets scarlet and ruined the bed. The Dozen wanted to be born, so they came early. One of the male nurses at the hospital passed out. Well, men aren't cut out to be nurses, are they? The doctor rushed Quartz into surgery. She was white as chalk, but she kept saying: "Don't let my babies die."

That's how big her heart is. She would die for these babies. Her heart breaks for them. She visits the ones at the cemetery twice a year. The ones from other sets that didn't come to term have little graves with baby bonnets carved into the stones. Precious as can be.

So what you're talking about, what that prosecuting attorney is talking about, that's the 'abomination.' It's evil to take away a woman's babies when they mean more to her than anything on earth. That's nothing but an injunction against motherhood, or against nature herself. The U.S. government and the state can take a woman's children away, but thank God they can't get an injunction against her blessed womb. As long as that's true, Quartz will fight the good fight, bringing these tiny angels into this cruel world to teach it right from wrong, just the way our Lord and Savior intended.

That's why Quartz does what she does. And that's why the ten of us, the ones that care for these blessed children, have offered our bodies to the sacred cause. We get down on our knees and thank the doctor for his goodness. Come spring there will be a celebration, and Heaven will rejoice to send these new babies of ours, maybe as many as sixty or seventy, into the world.

I still have my babysitting job, but now I'm part of something much bigger. Don't get me wrong. I've had sorrows. My first set of babies was stillborn. I think about them every day, and they give me the courage to go on. I thought about a burial at the cemetery with Quartz's babies, but I couldn't let them go. I felt like they wanted to stay with me, here in my room. This one is June Bug. See how tiny her ears are? And this one is Baby Ben. And here's Little Jillian. And this one with no arms is named Rudy.

So I've got my job with Quartz. And I've got my new job, which isn't a burden like those hateful bloggers say it is. How can you call it a burden to take part in the glory of God's creation? I'm alive to that glory, every wonderful day of my life. Amen.

Heroes and Villains

by
Michael Montoure

Ben turned sideways, edging through the narrow space in the hall. No other sound, here, but his breathing, the blood rushing in his ears, and the lazy drone of flies. Everything else was deadened by boxes and piles of crap, newspapers and magazines, vinyl records, books. Stacked to the ceiling. All of it seemed like it would come crashing down on him if he took one wrong step.

God, what if there was an earthquake? Could you imagine getting caught in here if there was a fire? He told himself to keep breathing.

Not that he wanted to breathe in here. The hot summer air was so heavy with the smell of old cigarettes, flat beer, and spoiled food that he would almost swear he could see it, a yellow-brown tinge to the few shafts of and gaps between boxes stacked in front of the windows.

"Please tell me all of these are bagged and boarded," he whispered to no one. "Bagged, at least. Or we'll never get the smell out."

He found more longboxes. No way he could reach all the way to the top of the stack, but, with a struggle, he managed to get one of them loose from the pile. He dropped it to the floor, swearing and manhandling the boxes above so they wouldn't topple over on to him.

Panting, he kneeled down and pulled the lid off the box. Bagged, yes, some of them boarded. He pulled out a small stack of comics and started flipping through them. No order to them, no system at all — dime-a-dozen variant-cover Image comics from the Nineties dumped in the same box with a few Golden Age titles he'd only ever seen pictures of on websites.

Gary was going to have a coronary when he saw all this. When he'd sent them out here to appraise the collection, he didn't know it was this big. No idea. No way to tell how many boxes were in the whole house. Dozens, easily, maybe hundreds? Enough to make the Mile High collection look like a spinner rack at Barnes and Noble.

"Have you seen this?" said the excited voice behind him.

"For Chrissakes, Paulie, keep your voice down," Ben stage-whispered. "Or we'll never talk her into a good price for all this."

"Okay, yeah, I know, but have you *seen* this?" Paulie repeated a little more quietly. "She's got *Dark Justice* number one! First goddamn printing! Look!"

He thrust the comic at Ben. It was nowhere near Mint condition — Fine or Very Good at best. Not worth hundreds, but fifty bucks at least.

"That's pre-Comics Code Authority. They had him, like, breaking bad guys' necks and shit like that," Paulie said. "So awesome. I am the stroke of midnight! I am the spirit of vengeance! I am Dark Justice!"

Ben laughed. "Yeah, it's cool, but, here, put it in this." He dumped one of the Image comics out of its sleeve and carefully took the comic from Paulie. "Where'd you find it? Are there more?"

"*Tons* more."

"Show me," Ben said, and followed him through the crooked house.

* * *

Hours later, well after dark, Ben was exhausted. Paulie

still seemed energized, like a kid on Christmas morning. *He's nineteen, he's just five years younger than me, but some days it feels more like twenty.*

"We didn't manage to go through everything," Ben told Mrs. Grant apologetically.

"Oh, I didn't think you would," she said. "Not in one day. He had so many comics, my David." She looked distant. "He's dead now, you know."

"Yes, Gary told us that. Our store manager, I mean, the man you talked to on the phone." Ben reached for the right thing to say. "I'm very sorry for your loss."

"Oh, thank you. It was his time, poor David. It's this house, really. He kept saying we'd move someday, but this house has a way of holding onto people, just as much as it holds on to things. I keep trying to sort out some of his things, and, well, some of my things too, I suppose, but — it all just gets away from you, doesn't it?" She still smiled, but tears were welling in her eyes. "I keep trying."

"Well, you came to the right place," Ben said. "I'm sure we can come to an arrangement."

Gary would never let a find like this slip out of his fingers. He might have to take out a business loan. Hell, he might need to move into a bigger storefront, but he'd find a way —

"I know they're worth some money, at least, aren't they?" she said. "Would... would five thousand be too much to ask?"

From behind him came Paulie's startled yelp, "Five thousand?"

He shut up when Ben, smiling and calm, took a small step backwards and his heel came down hard on Paulie's foot.

"That *is* too much, isn't it?" she said sheepishly.

Ben's mind reeled. He hadn't looked through a tenth of the comics, and he knew he'd seen over five thousand dollars' worth already, easy.

"Well, it *is* a lot of money," Ben said, "but I'm sure we

can manage to make you an offer. It's too late to reach my manager, but I'm sure he'll be back to you tomorrow." He'd wanted to call Gary earlier, but his cell phone had no signal in that house.

He had a sudden horrible thought. "Have you talked to anyone else about these? Any other offers on the table?"

"Oh, no, no one else. Are there even any other comic book stores in town?"

"No, I don't think so," Ben said, thinking of at least half-a-dozen. "We'll call you tomorrow, Mrs. Grant. It was very nice meeting you." *Very nice indeed.*

* * *

Paulie didn't shut up the whole way back to the bus stop. Ben mostly nodded and grunted in response. He stared off at nothing. This was huge. Gary had talked about giving them bonuses for handling this, but now — how big a bonus? A promotion? Maybe he'd finally talk the bastard into making him assistant manager. *That* would be something.

"Still can't believe they had all those old school *Dark Justice* issues," Paulie said. "That is my favorite character of all time. Seriously, all time." As if Ben couldn't tell that from half the T-shirts Paulie wore to work.

"Uh-huh," Ben said.

"And five grand for the whole goddamn thing! I cannot *wait* to see the look on Gary's face when we —" Paulie stopped in mid-sentence and dead in his tracks. "Do we *have* to tell him?" he said slowly.

"*What*?" Ben stared at him. "What the fuck are you talking about?"

Paulie's eyes were almost as wide as his glasses. "No, seriously, listen — Gary doesn't have, like, a legal claim on those books right now, right? He hasn't made an offer or anything, yet, right?"

"Okay, so?"

"Just saying, she wouldn't know if she was selling to the store — or to *us*. She wouldn't care, even. Ben, think about it. That's enough comics back there to start our *own* comics store with."

"Holy shit." Ben wanted to sit down. He settled for sinking backward against the nearest newspaper box to lean against it. "You're right."

"We could do it," Paulie said. "Seriously. Five thousand dollars isn't *that* much money." His voice broke a little when he said it, but he looked determined. "We each come up with half of it, go in on it together. Partners. Don't go into work tomorrow. Tell Gary you're sick, you quit, tell him anything, just don't tell him what we found. We get the money and come back here instead. Okay? What do you think — deal?"

Ben did the math in his head. *He's right. We could do it. I've got almost two thousand in savings. I'm sure I can borrow some money from Zeke or Tommy, or hell, even Mom. But no way I could come up with five thousand all by myself.*

He shook Paulie's hand. "Deal."

Something felt like it shifted, in that moment, like his whole world tilted off axis, just slightly. As Paulie gripped his hand tight, and their eyes locked, the world kept spinning. Ben leaned back uneasily. *It's that damn house. Being in that damn house all day is just getting to me, that's all.*

"This is my bus," Paulie said, looking past Ben's shoulder. "I'll call you later, all right? I'll call you. Oh my God, this'll be so awesome." He held up his hand for a high-five, and Ben awkwardly managed one. "I'll call you," Paulie kept saying, and waving, and grinning his head off as he ran for the bus.

Ben walked the rest of the distance to the bus stop, still a little off-balance. His own store. That was all he'd wanted since he was nine years old. So much to think about. This would give them stock to open with, but they'd have to come up with money for the space. They'd need a business license, insurance, a ton of paperwork and fees he probably didn't even know about, but — this was the start. A new life.

He sat down on the bus stop bench, dizzy with it all. He could get a better apartment. Maybe finally keep a girlfriend for more than six months. No more taking the bus — he could get his dad's old '89 Camaro up and running for the first time since it was his.

His very own comics store.

He frowned.

Well, mine and Paulie's.

That didn't sound as good, somehow.

What the hell kind of business partner is Paulie going to make, anyway? He's just a kid, for God's sake. This is the first smart idea he'd ever had in his life. He still plays with the toys and action figures at Gary's when he thinks no one's looking. His voice still almost breaks when he gets too excited about something, which is all the damn time.

Is this really someone I can walk into a bank with and ask for a business loan? Will Paulie be able to make tough decisions, like when Gary had had to fire Jordan for stealing shit? He shook his head, staring at the ground. He saw a rock near his foot and kicked it out into the street.

If only I'd thought of it first. I could've kept the idea to myself. But no, I need Paulie for this, no way I could raise five —

He looked up suddenly.

No, I couldn't... What about Paulie? We shook on it. We've got a deal.

He shook his head, disgusted. *A deal? Come on. Grow up.*

He pulled his cell phone out of his pocket, dialed a number. *A store of my own.*

"Hey, Zeke — sorry, I know it's getting late. Listen, you know how you always said if I ever changed my mind about selling the Camaro, I should tell you first? Well — you still interested?"

* * *

Ben stayed up late that night, unable to sleep. Paulie called him, a few times, but he turned the ringer off and let it go to voice mail. He was busy, looking at commercial real estate listings. Christ, he'd had no idea it was that expensive. No wonder Gary was always so stressed at the end of every month. And he played around in Photoshop, coming up with ideas for logos. Atomic Comics, was the name he'd settled on. Big bold Fifties font, bright colors, a rocketship in the background. Very retro.

He finally fell into bed and woke just three hours later to the alarm he'd set, a whole hour earlier than if he'd actually been getting up to go to work. Lots to do. He had a car to sell, and storage space and a moving truck to rent.

Paulie caught up with him at the old woman's house, as he and Zeke and Tommy and a few other guys he'd promised pizza and beer to were hauling boxes out to the truck. He was starting to realize that the storage unit he got this morning was only going to be big enough for maybe half the comics, but he'd figure something out for the rest.

Ben knew he looked terrible, but Paulie looked like shit. He clearly hadn't slept at all. He looked kinda feverish and shaky.

"I got the money," he said, holding out a check.

Ben glanced at it. It had a fancy floral-print, probably his mom's.

Ben grunted as he lifted a box into the truck. "Oh, yeah? Cool, that's great."

"What's..." Paulie looked around at all the activity, like a kid would stare at the bugs underneath a rock. "What's going on?"

Ben walked back toward the house. "What does it look like?"

"She's letting us take the comics before we even pay her?"

Ben sighed and stopped. "No. I paid her already, this afternoon. The whole five grand."

"Oh." Paulie stared at the check in his hand. "So — I pay you my half? I can change this — "

"No. Look, Paulie — just go home, okay?"

The look of comprehension that dawned over Paulie's face was almost horrible to watch. Ben couldn't help thinking he looked like the guy in the last panel from some old issue of "Tales from the Crypt."

"You can't. This was...this was my idea! You can't just —" He stared at the check in his hand and looked up at Ben with wide, wild eyes. "I got the money! I did! Do you know what I had to do? Do you know what I *did?*"

"Just go home."

"I can't ever go home! Don't you see that? This is — this is just —"

"What — unfair?"

Paulie shook his head. He stared deep into Ben's eyes, his hands balled into fists.

"Evil," Paulie said, and he sounded so serious when he said it that Ben wanted to laugh. But when he opened his mouth, the sound caught in his throat. He could only stand and watch, open-mouthed, as Paulie stormed off.

* * *

Late that night, as the last couple slices of pizza grew cold, and his friends cracked jokes and tried to one-up each other with bullshit stories, Ben stood up without a word, stretched, and reached for his jacket.

"Hey, man, you taking off?" Tommy said.

"Yeah, I'm gonna go cash out my tab. You guys want another pitcher of beer or anything?"

Tommy glanced around. "Naah, I think we're good," he

said. "You okay?"

"Tired."

"Long day," Zeke agreed.

"*Damn* long day. Thanks again, guys."

To be honest, something *was* bothering him. Paulie, of course. He hadn't been able to get his words out of his head all night:

I can't ever go home.

What the hell did that mean? What did that have to do with anything? It bugged him on the whole bus ride home. The words and the look on Paulie's face. When his bus passed Paulie's house, Ben swore under his breath and reached for the cord to ring the bell. He got off the bus and backtracked. Even though it was full on dark out, the air was still hot and unpleasantly heavy and wet.

He turned up the walkway to Paulie's house. *I can't ever go home,* Paulie said in his head. When Ben got close to Paulie's house, he saw that the front door was standing a couple of inches ajar.

That...didn't look right. Nobody just leaves their door standing open like that.

Leave. Just turn around, leave, get on the next bus that comes and don't look back. Call the police.

And tell them what? That he was freaked out by a door?

"Hello?" he said, and his own voice was so quiet even he could hardly hear it. He reached an uneasy finger out to the doorbell and then let his arm drop back to his side.

I'll call him. He dug the phone out of his pocket.

Oh, right — he left me all these voice messages last night. I should maybe listen to those before I talk to him. He thumbed through the list, deleted the ones from Gary, realizing he never had called in with an excuse for missing work. He pressed play on the first message from Paulie and held the phone up to his ear.

"Hey, it's me," Paulie's voice told him. "Still trying to figure out where the hell I'm gonna come up with the money. I knew I had some savings bonds or something like that my grandparents gave me, but it's not enough — and I looked it up online, and you have to wait for them to mature or something or they're not hardly worth anything. Do you know if there's some way around that, maybe? Call me back."

Next. "Hey, it's Paulie. I just talked to my Grandpa to see if he knew how the bonds worked, and to see if maybe he could loan me some more money and he bitched at me about how those bonds were for college and how I had to stop living in a dreamworld. He's awesome. Anyway, I'm gonna bite the bullet and ask my mom if she can loan me the money. I'll call you and let you know how it goes."

Ben knew none of this was happening right now, but he almost felt like if he stared hard enough through the darkened windows, he'd be able to look back through time. See Paulie pacing in his room.

Next. "Ben, listen, it's Paulie? Can you call me back? I need you to talk to my mom for a minute —" He could hear a woman's voice in the background, shouting and indistinct. Without even thinking about it, Ben reached up and gently pushed on the door, and it swayed quietly open under his touch.

"She keeps telling me this is *stupid,* and I just need you to talk to her for a minute, tell her this is *not* stupid, that we've got — we've got a *legitimate investment opportunity* here and I just need you to — can you please just call me — hang on —" Rustling sounds, and Paulie's muffled shouting —"Mom! Mom, I'm on the *goddamn phone!* Can you please just —" More rustling, and then Paulie's clear, flat voice — "I need to call you back."

Ben stepped inside the house, dreamlike, disconnected from this moment, riveted to the sounds of the night before. The inside of the house was as dark as the outside. A dim light came from down the hall, from the kitchen. He moved toward it silently.

Next. This next message had no words at all. Just the

sound of Paulie crying. Just deep, racking sobs. Ben had never heard anything like it, not from Paulie, not from anyone. It barely even sounded like a person. At the end of it all, it sounded like Paulie was trying to collect himself to say something, but instead he hung up.

Ben drifted along the corridor, drawn moth-like toward the light. *What did you do? Paulie, what did you do*? He steadied and guided himself by trailing the outstretched fingers of one hand along the wall. The orange-peel texture was cool and comforting under his fingertips.

He squinted at the harsh rectangle of light on his phone. One more message. He pressed 'next' again.

"Ben? Can you pick up the phone? Can you please, please, please just call me back?" He was sobbing. It was hard to make out the words. "Can you — I *fucked up*, Ben, this is — *bad*, this is *so bad*, I can't tell you on the phone, but — can you please, please come over here? Right now?"

There was more, but Ben didn't hear it. He forgot the phone was in his hand.

He was too busy staring at the open refrigerator in the dark kitchen, the broken glass and bent metal that had been its shelves. Broken condiment jars spilled into the pool of blood on the floor, under the body of a middle-aged woman — sprawled in the middle of it all. Her head was — Ben had never seen —

Blunt force trauma, was the technical phrase that drifted through his head, with no single coherent thought to attach itself to.

Ben stared, his mind a blank page, for one timeless moment.

The next thing he knew he'd bolted to the sink, just barely in time for all that pizza and beer to come back on him. When he finally stopped, he ran water in the sink, groped around, and found the switch for the garbage disposal. He stood there, gasping for breath, then wandered away from the sink, tap and disposal still running, forgotten.

Oh, Paulie. Paulie, you really have fucked up this time.

Was he really not here? Had he really run out of the house — no, stolen his dead mother's checkbook and then run out of the house, and just not looked back? Just hoped the problem would go away? What, and left all his stuff here?

Ben made it out to the hallway and finally thought to turn on a light. He made his way up the stairs to Paulie's room.

The door to Paulie's room stood wide open, and a single floor lamp lit the room. Ben stood staring in the doorway.

"Holy fuck."

The poster spread across the wall had a glaring masked face and huge blood red letters. 'I am the voice of the night. I am the answer to the cries of the innocent. I am justice — Dark Justice!'

He never used to have all this stuff. There were other posters along with it, all of them Dark Justice. Like the toys and action figures on the nightstand, the mini-statues and busts — Wait, they used to have that one at the store, that was like a couple hundred dollars, how the hell did Paulie ever afford —

"You little shit," Ben whispered, stepping inside. He knew. All this stuff — this was what Gary had fired Jordan for stealing, but it hadn't been Jordan doing it. Paulie's favorite character — why hadn't Gary figured it out?

Ben looked around wildly. He knew he had to get out of here — he'd half-forgotten the body downstairs, seeing all this, but his nerves were still screaming at him. But first, he had to do something about this, get all of it back to Gary. He spotted a cardboard box full of magazines and mail. He dumped it out on the bed and started gathering the toys and figures into it —

And then the light in the room suddenly spun and

shifted in a crazy arc, and Ben had just a second to wonder what the hell was happening before Paulie swung the lamp like a baseball bat into the side of his head.

The box fell out of his hands and crashed to the floor. He dropped to his knees, reaching up into his hair, fingers touching blood and broken glass. He barely had time to think Paulie's name before his eyes fell shut, and he pitched forward onto the floor.

* * *

He woke up, with something covering his eyes, his arms trapped, but knew immediately where he was. The smell of that old house, the flat beer and ancient smoke was distinct like a fingerprint. And something else, something new, a sharp scent that made him think of summer —

"I am the spirit of vengeance," a voice said.

Ben pulled against whatever was holding him. Plastic? Plastic wrap, it felt like, wrapped around him, binding him to a chair. *Bagged and boarded.* A strange giggle slipped loose from somewhere deep inside him.

"I am the answer to the cries of the innocent."

"Paulie? What the fuck, man? Get me out of this."

The duct tape over his eyes was suddenly ripped away.

"I," the voice said, "am Dark Justice!"

So it was. The cheap Halloween costume version, at least.

Paulie glared down at him through masked eyes, standing in a way that made him seem as if he were trying to make himself broader and taller.

"Fuck, *really?*" Ben said.

"You stand accused," Dark Justice said, "of fraud, deception, betrayal. And now theft!" His voice was a low and unconvincing growl. "I have found you guilty. Your time has come to face Justice!"

"Paulie, come on, knock it off. This shit isn't funny."

Dark Justice took a step backwards. "I'm...you are... mistaken. I am...I am not..." Paulie tore the mask off. "Shit. You recognized my voice, didn't you? Why didn't I *think* of that?" He smacked himself hard in the forehead with the heel of his hand. "Stupid, *stupid*." He looked around, pacing like a caged animal. "Listen, I was just going to scare you, make you watch this shit burn."

"Burn?" Ben's eyes darted around. And now he saw them, empty cans of lighter fluid on top of boxes and boxes of comics. "You crazy little — wait, where's Mrs. Grant?"

"Oh, she's *here*," Paulie said, giggling. "She's here. She's part of this whole collection, now. She's not going anywhere ever again. I made sure of that."

Ben pulled against the plastic wrap. It was stretching, loosening, and Paulie hadn't bound his legs. "Paulie, listen, let's talk about this —"

"Too late." Paulie pulled the mask back on. "I was just gonna scare you, but now, I can't let you go. I have to get away from here. I have to start over. I have to *do* this. I really have to do this. It's all I have left. But you *know*."

"I know? What?"

"My secret identity. You can't tell anybody." He reached into a pocket of the cheap vinyl utility belt and pulled out a Zippo lighter. "There are people like you everywhere and I'm going to find them. Goodbye, Ben."

He flipped the lighter open.

Ben was up and out of his chair, pulling his arms free of the last shreds of plastic. He dived full on at Paulie and knocked him to the floor, landing on top of him.

Ben kneeled on Paulie's breastbone, crushing the breath out of him. He hadn't thrown a punch in years, not since fights back on the playground, but it all came back to him. He pounded on Paulie's face with both fists. Right, left, right.

"Bam!" Ben shouted. "Pow! How do you like your superhero bullshit now, huh? Huh?! You crazy little *shit*!"

Ben grabbed the lighter and stood up, panting. Paulie

wasn't moving. He was just laying there, his breath coming in broken sobs.

Ben looked around to see how bad the damage was. Bad. Paulie'd poured lighter fluid on every goddamn box, decades of comics, treasure and trash alike, all ruined, worthless.

Ben was so mad he couldn't see straight, couldn't focus on anything. Swearing under his breath, he flipped open the lighter and brought it to life. "Fight your way out of this, Dark Justice," he said, as he tossed the lighter onto the nearest box, and started edging sideways down the hall, toward the exit.

Or away from the exit!

This was a dead-end. Maybe there was more corridor on the other side of these boxes, maybe a wall...He couldn't tell. *Which way did we come in?* He backtracked, getting closer than he wanted to the flames that were already leaping and dancing, spreading to the yellowed wallpaper.

There — there, that's the kitchen, with all those stacks of garbage bags, if I can just get past that, out into the hallway, I'll end up —

Back where Paulie was. He didn't look like he was breathing.

The smoke was getting to Ben. How had he gone in a circle? How was that fucking possible?

This house has a way of holding onto people, Mrs. Grant had said. Just as much as it holds on to things.

Ben tried again, a different path. He found a door, but the knob was too hot to hold on to. The door was burning to the touch. He had to turn around again, and this is where Paulie was, wasn't it? Where was he now?

"Paulie? Where are you?" Ben shouted, but raising his voice just made him cough more. It was getting hard to see.

Laughter rang out from somewhere. From everywhere at once. Ben heard the voice coming from down halls, from behind doors —"I am the darkness before dawn!" It wasn't even recognizable as Paulie, anymore, not even human. "I am the spirit of vengeance, the fires of hell!"

Except for the roaring of the fire and the crashing of the beams, that was the last sound he heard before the crooked house came tumbling down.

Let Them into Your Heart

by
Lee Widener

He was watching me. I was pretty sure. Although he seemed as if he were trying to be inconspicuous, I was a dedicated people watcher, and I could tell when someone was watching and waiting for something to happen. The question was, why was he watching me? I got the answer when I threw a candy wrapper in the garbage basket.

He was sitting on the bench on the other side of the basket and as soon as the wrapper landed, his hand snaked out and neatly retrieved the candy wrapper, depositing it into the cloth bag at his side.

Without so much as a glance my way, he moved to another bench a little farther down and began watching two teenage girls. They were chattering away, texting on their cell phones, and eating candy bars. When they finished, they blithely threw the wrappers on the ground and walked off. He casually reached down, picked up the candy wrappers, and put them in his bag.

The man made a circuit around the park, inspecting the garbage baskets, checking the ground and bushes. He never picked up anything but candy wrappers.

A few days later, the next time I had lunch in the park, I saw him again. I took out a chocolate bar. Even though he was already perched next to someone else, he noticed me. Our eyes met, and I felt like we were dueling. He looked away when a woman placed an empty candy bag in a brown paper bag and threw the whole thing into the garbage basket.

He scooted over to the garbage basket, opened the bag, and snatched up the candy wrapper.

Trying to keep his attention, I ate my chocolate bar deliberately, slowly. I set the wrapper down next to me and took out a book.

The old man hustled over to my bench and sat down. He glanced at the wrapper on the bench, bent over to pull up his socks, and then sat gazing at the sky.

"Hello," I said, in my most unassuming manner, "Nice day."

He half way stood up, but then changed his mind and sat back down. "Um... yes," was his only reply.

What had appeared as a smart, green tweed sport coat from a distance revealed itself, upon closer inspection, to be frayed at the cuffs. The lining poked through at the elbows. His black sneakers were coming apart, but the black beret he wore seemed relatively new. I decided to be bold.

"You like candy wrappers," I said.

He looked at me, as if confused. "What do you mean?"

"Well, I've been watching you. You pick up all the candy wrappers around here." I held out my chocolate bar wrapper. "Would you like this one?"

Without saying a word, he took the wrapper and stowed it in his bag.

I held out my hand. "I'm Harold."

He stared at my hand as if nobody had offered him this form of friendship in a long time. After a moment he took my hand and shook it. From the look of the wrinkles on his face, I judged his age to be about seventy years old.

"Hampton," he mumbled.

"So, why do you collect candy wrappers?" I asked, "You're obviously not on a mission to clean up the world or you wouldn't be so selective."

"Art," he said. "I'm an artist."

"Really?" I was intrigued. "You make art from candy wrappers?"

"Yes." His attention wandered. He glanced around, possibly looking for more cast aside candy wrappers.

"I write for an art publication. The idea of art made from candy wrappers piques my interest."

"A writer. About art." I could see the look of doubt on his face.

"Yes. I work for *Art Beat*. Our office is just on the other side of the park."

"Art Beat. I've seen that." His eyes moved up and down examining me closer.

I took a business card from my pocket. "I'd like to keep in touch."

He took the card and glanced at it before slipping it into a pocket inside his faded jacket.

"Is your work on display anywhere? I'd like to see it."

"No. World doesn't care... about... real art."

"I care. I'm very interested. I'd like to see your work."

For a minute he looked like he was going to run, gripping the side of the bench, ready to take off, but eventually he got control of himself. A gleam came into his eyes. I didn't want to press too hard, but I was excited at the prospect, however slim, of discovering a unique artist.

"My car is parked over at the office. We could go now, and see your work, if that would be convenient."

"Not now. Have work to do. Tonight."

He took my card out of his pocket and wrote an address on the back.

"Eight o'clock. Don't be late," he said, handing me the card.

"I wouldn't miss this appointment for the world." I placed the card back in my pocket. When I looked up, he was half way across the park, searching for more candy wrappers.

Later that night, as I was getting ready to visit what could possibly be a fascinating new discovery for the world of art, or even more possibly, a crazy old man with a bunch of candy wrappers glued onto pieces of paper, I allowed myself a slight glimmer of hope. The magazine needed a discovery, something unique. I checked the address Mr. Hampton had written on the back of my card. To my surprise, it wasn't an address in Felony Flats, as people were wont to call the part of town where derelicts lived. It was an address in a gentrified factory district renowned for its artist's studios. I wondered if any of the artists I knew in the area were acquainted with Mr. Hampton.

I had no trouble finding the neighborhood. I'd been there many times before. Finding his address was more difficult. I parked my car in a nearly deserted lot. The door to his studio turned out to be down a back alley beside an old brick warehouse. It was a barren, lonely area. I knocked on the door. The sound of my raps seemed to be swallowed in the desolation. I got no answer. Knocking again, louder, I wondered if I should turn around and go home. The promise of a glorious new artistic find lured me on. I pushed on the heavy metal door, and it swung open, the smell of stale air and mold assaulting me. With trepidation, I inched through the door.

Inside, I was met by a hallway painted industrial green, and dotted with wooden doors locked with padlocks. A dimly lit stairway led to the bowels of the building. A black arrow pointed down. A sign proclaimed B 1-5. I checked the address Hampton had written, and sure enough, it said B5. I wasn't sure I wanted to be here. What if Hampton was some crazy murderer waiting to slit my throat? I started down the stairs, each step creaking ominously as I cautiously set foot upon it. This whole place could come apart at any minute.

At the bottom of the stairs, a solitary bulb suspended from the ceiling barely lit the way. Shadows ate the walls and floor. I resisted the urge to turn and flee. I was a big boy. I didn't need to be afraid of being alone at night in the basement of a creepy old building. At the far end of the hall was one lone door. Reaching for the wall, I crept forward. I could hear music coming from the other side of the door. It was Holst's *The Planets*.

The sign on the door, made of candy wrappers folded into various shapes and letters portrayed a pastoral landscape with a sleek spaceship floating in the sky. Letters in the sky spelled out the slogan 'Do Not Fear Them.' The artistry was really quite amazing.

I knocked on the door and to my surprise it opened immediately. Hampton stood inside eying me with bemusement. I held out a basket filled with gourmet candy. He let a grin slip across his face and grunted at me.

"Come in."

Stepping into the room, I wasn't sure what to expect – a regular artist's studio, paint spattered everywhere; a moldy old hovel housing a penniless derelict, a stark and barren edifice? What greeted me could have been mistaken for a well-kept apartment anywhere in the city. As I looked around the comfortably appointed room, I found no trace I was in the basement of an old warehouse. This room had the look of an old retired man's living room – an easy- chair was situated before a television. An end table next to the chair held a plate from a recently eaten meal. Hampton softly closed the door behind me and set the basket of candy on an expensive looking antique writing desk.

"Good stuff," he said, indicating the basket. "Foil wrap is hard to find."

"This is a nice place you have. Not what I was expecting at all."

"I wear rags when I go gathering for safety. Nobody bothers an old bum who goes through the garbage."

"Indeed. Smart move."

He gestured for me to follow him.

"But I'm not an old bum. I worked as long as they would let me. Now I live on a pension. Come, I'll show you the operation."

We entered another room with a curtain for a door. It was filled with high metal shelving units, a long worktable, and an industrial sink. A couple of garbage bags sat next to the door. Some of the shelves overflowed with various art supplies; paper, boards, bottles and bottles of glue. Other shelves held box after box of candy wrappers, each wrapper carefully flattened and sorted by type of candy and color.

The table was heaped with rumpled candy wrappers. From one side of the table rose a stack of bricks wrapped in fabric. On top of the sink rested a stack of neatly folded rags.

"This is where it all begins," he said. "All the recently gathered wrappers come in here so I can clean them. Even wrappers that look clean have to wiped off. They have food particles that attract bugs. Bugs are not good. Also, They like things to be clean. After I clean them, I flatten them. After flattening, they're sorted – type of candy and color. They like things to be orderly. Raw materials for art."

"Very impressive."

He led me into another room. This one had a large wooden table with a multitude of candy wrappers strewn about, along with scissors, a variety of X-Acto knives, canisters of glue and other art supplies. There was a shelf in the corner that held a collection of old record albums and a turntable. "Vinyl is much better than that digital crap." Hampton crossed the room and turned the record over. "Fuller spectrum. They like that."

He placed the needle on the edge of the disc and lush classical music filled the room. The old man then turned a rheostat on the wall, and a collection of lights on the ceiling lit up and began rotating above a multicolored plastic contraption that filled the room with waves of ever changing colored light. "This is where I create. The colors help me connect to Their energy."

So he was a crazy old crackpot after all. "Their energy?" I inquired.

"*The Ones Who Talk*. They gave me my mission, my purpose and my talent."

I moved closer to examine the table. The picture in progress appeared to be of a face floating in the clouds assembled from small Bit-o-Honey wrappers. I hadn't seen those in years. Uncomfortably, I fancied the face looked a bit like my own.

"Tell me more," I invited, not really sure I wanted to hear more. "Your... mission?"

"Now you're sure I'm some crazy fanatic. Maybe, I don't

care. Life's not boring anymore. They first spoke shortly after I retired." He picked up a book from the table and caressed it. "Reading Virginia Woolf, a phrase electrified me. 'I don't like human nature unless all candied over with art.' She was right. Except for art, there's not much about humanity to like. Then They spoke. Get candy. Make art. Tried not to listen, but They were insistent. I started collecting candy wrappers. Better for art than candy itself. They agreed. They're not unreasonable."

This was getting a little deep for me, and the colored lights were starting to make me dizzy, but after taking the trouble to come all the way out here, I wanted to see the art. "Do you have any of your work here?"

"Course I do. Where else would it be?" He left the room and went farther down the hall. I followed him to another door. Screaming from the door was the word "Gallery," in an ornate script, made entirely of folded silver and gold foil candy wrappers. It was exquisite handiwork. The old man smiled at me. "Get ready," he warned, pushing open the door.

A faint smell of sweetness wafted from the room. He reached his hand inside and twisted another rheostat on the wall. The undulating pattern of colored lights illuminated the room. What I saw when I stepped into the room, for the first time in my life, made my jaw drop. I was speechless. I was dumbfounded.

What lay before me was a room, at least thirty feet square, full of brightly colored, glimmering objects, furniture included, apparently made completely from candy wrappers. I timidly walked a few steps into the room, trying to take it all in. The wall to the right was one large mural depicting an alien landscape, complete with tall, spired buildings, a yellow and pink sky, and a number of gray-skinned humanoid figures waving hello. Covering the left wall were tiny waxy papers approximately three inches square. When I went closer, I discovered they were Bazooka Joe bubblegum comics. The floor was an intricately woven carpet of wrappers displaying a spiral mandala. The ceiling was a dark purple and black night sky, complete with shimmering planets and stars.

Filling the room were all manner of furniture and sculptures, each one seemingly constructed of nothing but candy wrappers and boxes. I saw a small table, a bed, a bookshelf filled with what looked to be books, and yes, when I took one off the shelf it had a cover made from flattened candy boxes and page after candy wrapper page, each one a different illustration. I estimated over a hundred of these books crammed the shelf. A couple of the gray-skinned alien figures with big heads stood four feet tall, and from their positions, I could only surmise they were dancing with each other. Where did he find gray candy wrappers? In one corner sat, of all things, a bathtub, hardened with some kind of glue or something, as it was rigid to my touch.

The centerpiece of the entire room was what I could only describe as a throne. Intricate scrollwork adorned every inch of the eight foot tall chair. Every color in the rainbow wove in and out creating symmetrical patterns which seemed to pulsate under the ululating lights. Above the throne, across the back, stretched a banner that entreated, in more gold foil letters, "Let Them Into Your Heart." It was simply breathtaking. Where did he get all these candy wrappers? I turned to find Hampton. He was standing by the door, a faraway look in his eyes.

"There must be millions of candy wrappers here. Where do you get them all?"

"You've seen. Parks. Office lunchrooms. Anywhere people eat candy."

"But you can't get all that many that way..."

"You're right. Theater dumpsters are goldmines. Certain times of the year are key – the week after Halloween, Easter, Valentine's Day."

"Mr. Hampton, I'm simply floored. This is the most original collection of art I've ever seen. It must be shared with the world."

Hampton looked at the floor and chuckled to himself. "Glad you like it. They're glad too. But, you haven't heard the whole message yet. Haven't heard Them. These pieces are not just pretty. They have a purpose."

"A purpose?"

Hampton left the doorway and approached the throne. "Let me tell you. Have a seat." He motioned toward the throne.

"Oh, I couldn't."

"It's okay. It's strong. Very strong. I insist."

Doubtfully, I sat in the huge chair. It was surprisingly comfortable, but from where the throne sat the swirling lights on the ceiling were very bright. My head was swimming. I felt something on my right arm, and when I looked down, Hampton was fastening my arm to the chair with a strap made from Hershey's chocolate bar wrappers.

"Wait a minute," I tried to raise my arm.

Before I knew it, he had moved to the other side and was securing my left arm to the chair.

"Hey now, what's going on?"

Hampton had bent over and was now strapping my legs in place. I tried to stand up, but the chair was much stronger than you might expect of something constructed from paper and foil. Something held it to the floor.

"This isn't funny, Mr. Hampton. Let me up."

What the hell was he up to? What did I have with me I could use to get out of these straps? Had I brought anything with me I could use as a weapon? Why hadn't I let anyone know where I was going?

"Don't worry," Hampton cooed. "Everything will be fine in just a few moments. Do not fear Them. Let Them into your heart. That day when They first spoke, when I had been struck by that Virginia Woolf quote, They told me of their mission. There's so much strife in the world. So much unhappiness, pain. They want to end all that, and They can. Just need people to help them." From behind the throne Hampton produced the most artfully crafted tin foil hat I had ever seen and placed it on my head, fastening it with a strap under my chin. Immediately I felt a mild jolt of electricity through my body.

"See here, Hampton, this isn't funny," I said, trying to sound commanding. "Let me loose immediately."

"Look at the lights. You'll hear Them talk."

I didn't want to look at those lights, but I couldn't close my eyes. I was feeling decidedly dizzy. Electricity coursed through my body again. This time it was stronger. My vision blurred. I had to get out of here before something bad happened. I struggled, but my candy wrapper bonds were too strong. Electricity shot through my body again, and this time it was so strong my body convulsed. I was able to look away from the lights long enough to look down at myself. I was shocked to see the form of one of the gray-skinned alien creatures sitting on my lap. No... not on my lap... in the same space I was occupying, and it was transparent, like a ghost.

"I am here, Hampton."

"I am glad," Hampton answered.

"You have done well."

Who was Hampton talking to? That sounded like... like MY voice... but I wasn't talking!

"This will be a happy time," the voice said. MY voice! "When I share space with this one, we will bring much peace to this world."

"Do you hear It, Mr. Art Critic?" Hampton asked. "You're lucky. You get to Share. Look at the lights."

Involuntarily, my eyes rose to the twirling lights on the ceiling, and I felt a huge jolt of electricity. My tongue stuck out, my entire body shook, and I could feel my consciousness fading...

* * *

My eyes flickered open. What the hell? Had I been asleep? I turned my head to look around, and my neck felt stiff. I was sitting in the throne in Mr. Hampton's amazing candy wrapper art gallery. But, how did I get there? I didn't remember sitting down. I heard a shuffling noise to my right, and I turned to see Mr. Hampton entering the room with a glass of water.

"Good. You're awake," he said. "You passed out." He handed me the glass of water. "Careful not to spill. Feeling all right?"

I put my arm up to take the glass, and for a minute it seemed like there was another arm moving along with mine, a thin gray arm. I rubbed my eyes, and the image was gone. Draining the glass, I felt better.

"That's odd," I said. "I don't think that's ever happened before."

"Anyway. You like the art."

"My goodness, yes. It's the most exciting collection of art I think I've ever seen. We're going to want to do a feature on this. If I'm not mistaken, you're going to make a big splash in the art world. May I bring a couple of photographers over tomorrow?"

"Sure. The world needs a big splash."

I stood up, a little unsteady on my feet. I must have really crashed out. Making a mental note to visit the doctor, I held out my hand for Hampton to shake. Again I had the strange feeling there was another arm alongside mine. Hampton took my hand and gave it a single pump. His grip was incredibly strong for an old man. He saw me to the door and put his hand on my shoulder as I was leaving.

"You're a good man," he said. "You let *Them* into your heart."

In His Own Graven Image

by
Pete Clark

The creature was exactly as Harris had described. It stood, quiet and bowed, in the centre of the room. Both windows were closed and curtained, and within the room's dark confines, a rank sourness tainted air and mood alike. Harris stood a way off to the side, apparently in close conversation with the creature's owner, perhaps discussing fees and insurance excesses. The man stood as did his charge, with head bowed and the soft rhythmic rise and fall of his chest the only clear sign that he was alive. His face bore a look of worried perplexity.

Dauphin stood at the room's only door, his fingers describing unnatural configurations as they twisted and writhed. Sweat stood out on his brow like blood on a thorn-pricked brow. The creature moved suddenly, a great gassy shudder as it shifted its feet. Their sound on the rough weave of the carpet was deafening to Dauphin, for he had closed off all other noise, narrowed his eyes to stare at the thing in front of him with arrows of bright comprehension. He unconsciously twinned the creature's movement, stepping forward and then back again as the thing's eyes found his. There was a kind of blank recognition in them, as if it had been primed for this very moment. Dauphin let out a small noise, part revulsion and part ecstasy.

In the pockets of his too-large jacket lay a pair of powdered vinyl gloves and a Polaroid camera. He removed these and set them on a table to his left. Under the jacket he was naked, and he achieved this state now by shrugging the garment from his shoulders. Its size allowed it to fall easily, and it pooled around his feet. He stepped from it, an almost feminine gesture. The man who had led them here to his creature let an involuntary gasp of horror at the sight.

Dauphin's skin was lashed with scars from temple to ankle, livid cross hatchings that seemed to glow in the dullness of the room.

Dauphin spoke softly now to Harris, and the procurer broke from his conversation and crossed the room to where his boss stood naked. The warm air could do nothing to soften the nervous tautness of his skin across chest and stomach and scrotum. He breathed the sour air in tight little gasps, as if he needed the oxygen but none of the taste or smell of the creature that tainted it.

"I'm ready," he said.

Harris nodded and turned his attention back to the creature's owner, where he repeated the nod, this one with a beckoning flick of his wrist. The man stepped forward and laid a hand on the creature's head. It turned to him, a rattling purr in its throat. Harris laid his hand upon Dauphin's arm and gently encouraged him forward.

Dauphin knelt onto the rough carpet, not feeling the bite of fibre at his knees, feeling nothing now except a rush of pleasure which invariably accompanied acquisitions of this type. He shut his eyes slowly, using his hands to feel the familiar contours.

Every inch was a topography of scarification; keloid ridges every shade of red from maroon to faintest pink. There were huge white slashes across his back, old scars from a time before he had learned control, before he had yearned for order and classification. As the scars followed the bony ridges of his body, over his shoulders and down the jut of his chest, they darkened in colour and thus showed their younger age. These were more orderly, smaller and set so as to render pattern and aesthetic surety. He had tiger-striped legs and buttocks. Set as punctuation for all of these major scars, were smaller, neater marks. These could only have been made by teeth, and closer study revealed sets of two, four and as many as twelve punctures per bite. There were none on the backs of his hands, although there was a pair worming around his wrists. These would jut from his sleeves, if he were wearing any, like the heads of tiny snakes.

He laid his hands on the carpet and opened his eyes. The creature had moved forward and was standing no more than four feet away now. His eyes widened at the sight of it this close. It resembled a chimpanzee in basic physiognomy, but one perhaps with cockerel and wolf in its lineage. A lurid violet comb of flesh ran the length of its flattened dome of a head, and split at the nape of its neck to flow back around the thing's shoulders, meeting at a knot of bruise-coloured gristle in the hollow of its throat. Its jaws were too elongated for ape, and too heavily furred. It dripped thick saliva from these jaws and wiped away the mess with a hand like bunched knives. Dauphin quivered from his position of supplication. The creature edged forward.

"Does it have a name, this one?" Dauphin asked gently. The man shook his head.

"I don't name them. It is a demon, a chupacabra, a gargoyle. It is whatever you want to name it."

Dauphin was satisfied, it seemed, for he reached for the thing's snout and stroked the fur there.

"Gargoyle," he whispered, and the thing knew its name. It growled.

Dauphin could feel the vibrations rising through the creature's body. He turned his own body, presenting his flank, and pointed to a spot of skin that was soft pink and devoid of scar tissue.

"Here," he whispered, and the man urged his charge forward and pointed to the spot. The thing needed no further encouragement, for it unleashed it knife claws and struck Dauphin with the fluid grace of a creature more suited to ambush hunting than chained servitude. A vicious snarl accompanied the attack, and as the creature drew back for a second swipe, Dauphin, as he always did, wondered if this

129

would be the last thing he felt. The razors parted air scant millimetres from his flesh, and the tight chink of chain being pulled taut cut through the sour air. The creature sat back on shit-stained haunches and extended a long tongue to lick Dauphin's blood from its claws. Harris rushed in with gloved hands to snap a Polaroid of the wound still leaking blood, and once done, pressed padded gauze to it. He proceeded to drag Dauphin back towards his discarded jacket. He had gone pale as snow, and as Harris helped him to dress, pressing adhesive tape across the pad of gauze as he did so, the creature's owner spoke.

"Why?" he asked.

"He collects them," Harris replied. On seeing the man's confusion, he added, "The scars."

* * *

The Polaroid joined the hundreds already pinned to the wall of Dauphin's office. They formed a tapestry of horrors. On show here were wounds made by every type of creature with claw or tooth. Dauphin wasn't foolish enough to believe he could gain a mark from every single species, but had captured one from each major group capable of harm. So here was the tooth mark from a big cat, a tiger. Next to that were dog, and bear and hyena, and wolverine. There were talon gouges from golden eagle and sparrow alike. A shark bite adorned his upper arm, and there were cuts and bites from insects, and from spiders, scorpions and a dozen species of snake. But these were everyday creatures and while they had their place, covering eighty percent of him, in fact, it wasn't these he was most proud of. There were others, like this newest adornment, the living gargoyle, which set his heart truly racing.

These were the Penny Blacks, the elusive Gauguin, or the Gutenberg Bible. They were the ones that he had been told he could never acquire, that no amount of money could force these creatures into being. But he had known the truth, and had ploughed his not inconsiderable fortune into the discovery of them. And so here, next to a long, winding scar made by the curving knife claw of a giant anteater, was a subtler mark. Shaped like a ring of raised pebbles, the mark left by the sucker of a giant kraken. And here, nestling among the ragged beak marks of a hundred-strong flock of starlings, a scar like a deep well, its originator, the talon of a thunderbird, the star of half a thousand cryptozoology websites. And yet these were not the strangest.

From chupacabra to demon, from vampire to were-creatures with a dozen or more lineages, all had their place. Creatures of fable and children's story had made their mark upon his old flesh, unicorn and devil alike. There was a three-tined scratch across his stomach where a poltergeist had been unable to resist the lure of touching skin, marking skin. That one, in which the deep wounds had appeared as if from the air itself, had had Dauphin reeling with ecstasy for a full week.

Dauphin looked upon his collection now, running a hand across a particular favourite Polaroid, finding its twin on himself, comparing the wound to the scar. The beauty in this collection, as Dauphin could see it, was that it only started with the wound. The ownership of such was fleeting, apt to vanish before you had a chance to peruse its stinging reality. Replaced with the scar, it formed a second longer lasting collection. Two for the price of one.

And what price? He had been bankrupted more than once, scratching his wealth back from the brink with well-placed share deals, and the sale of much of his family homes and land. He had money enough, he thought, for one last acquisition, and he was determined to make this the one to eclipse all his others. He wasn't such a fool as to forget that wrenching feeling when, each time he parted with money, each time the deal was made, he would turn to his procurer, the ever reliable Harris, and say, "After this, it ends, Harris. There cannot be any others. I cannot take it."

And yet here he was now, feeling the contours of his collection, feeling for that exquisite smoothness that would signal the discovery of another square inch of unmarked skin. He found it, of course, nestled high into the humid spot between thigh and scrotum. It would be there, this next one. He thought about taking a picture of that spot now, so that he would have a 'before' reference point, for this final time. He didn't, however. He could not go back and photograph each spot before its ruination, and he would not start now, so near the end.

* * *

"I have it," said Harris.

"You do?" Dauphin replied, eyebrows raised. His heart raced. "And is it....?"

"I am not sure which one will come," Harris said. "Only that one will."

"I have found the spot. The only spot left. This is the last, Harris. Truly the last."

"As you wish." Ever discreet, Harris neither asked nor showed interest. He procured. He bargained and haggled and begged on Dauphin's behalf, content to be the one who took the derisive looks, discovered and endured the harsh environs, and the beatings. He risked his life for Dauphin on a daily basis and had more than once been in jeopardy of losing it. His skin was similarly marked, although to a lesser degree, and there was none of the order and precise placing. None of the careful planning. For Harris, one scar, whether left by snake or wolf or porcupine quill, or perhaps something altogether more ethereal, was one too many. He did what he did for money.

"When?" asked Dauphin. Harris told him a date and venue. It was sufficiently far enough in the future for the fervour of anticipation to boil over in him, but not so far that he grew impatient and perhaps spoiled the blank area on his skin with a hasty purchase, something to soothe the impatient twitch in his hands and the irritation in his mind.

When that day finally arrived, Dauphin was at fever pitch,

his very marrow on fire with desire. The money had been paid (Harris did not say to whom, and Dauphin could not guess), and the line of zeros that made up his remaining bank balance was a mild irritation, but nothing more. After this, he thought, money would be rendered irrelevant.

The dockside loomed ahead, rusted and bulky containers forming high corridors of steel through which Dauphin and Harris threaded their way. The smell of brackish water and gull shit met them at every turn, but Dauphin was so mesmerised by the place and the secret it held, that he scarcely noticed. Harris was less involved, and so held a handkerchief over his nose and mouth. He directed Dauphin with muffled instructions, sometimes no more than a nod of the head.

The building they sought was unimpressive, given its purpose on this night. Squat and squalid in equal measure, the shape of it was partially obscured by darkness and partly by piles of rope and general flotsam. They made their way to it, Harris leading. Dauphin was wary now they had gotten this close. What if it was a fake, or worse, the real thing but not at all as he imagined or desired. Perhaps Dauphin's last scar would be the wound caused when his heart broke at the sight of it.

The door opened easily. They stepped into gloom so absolute it was like walking into tar. They both slowed their pace, shuffling forward to avoid tripping. A gleam of illumination washed across the room suddenly, the light from a passing freighter perhaps, and in its wake, Dauphin saw the layout of the room.

No windows, or none with glass that wasn't black with grime. A locker against one wall, its door limp on one hinge, its contents spilling like the organs at a dissection. A pair of overalls, a boot. There was a table, complete with cup and plate. A single chair.

The figure sitting at the table looked as human as Dauphin did himself. A short man, he looked, utterly still and utterly expressionless. Clothes hung on him like they had been draped across a wire frame, and his cheekbones

133

looked sharp enough to wound. He had short hair in an antique style, but he didn't look particularly out of place. In fact, it looked as though he rather suited the gloom, and was content to dwell there. As the light from the freighter crept across him, his eyes caught the gleam and threw it back at Dauphin in twin bright threads. He raised his head, the threads remaining steady, and looked at Dauphin.

He knew instantly that this was no fake. Had he expected whiteness, wings and feathery beauty to envelope him it its love? Perhaps, somewhere deep inside him. But this was the real thing, he had no doubt. The man stood, shaking off the gloom like rainwater from an overcoat, and approached Dauphin transformed, his own darkness gleaming somehow against the darkness of the room's interior. He appeared as though dipped in oil, light playing across him like a borealis.

Harris had retreated a few steps, and now a few more. Dauphin registered the sound but it meant nothing to him. The dark man continued his approach until he was mere feet away, and Dauphin spoke.

"Seraphim," he whispered and the dark man nodded. At this movement, shreds of darkness fell away, gleaming brightly as they went, like black fire. They pooled about him and ran like mercury until they met his feet, where they merged into him once more. "Ah," Dauphin said. "My seraphim."

The angel, for it truly was such, Dauphin knew, opened its mouth as if to speak. In the scant seconds before noise was heard, Dauphin's mind raced through half a hundred scenarios. He would be instantly deafened or killed outright. Perhaps he would have a revelation of such profundity that the sixty or so years he had lived on earth, and the forty of those he had dedicated to his collection, would be rendered irrelevant. Perhaps no sound would be heard, but only a subsonic tremor of such ferocity that he would be literally shaken to his marrow. None of these things happened. The thing's voice was quiet, pleasant, and calming. It soothed Dauphin's nerves instantly.

"You are Dauphin?" it asked.

To have his name spoken aloud by this thing, to hear the syllables flow from its tongue and lips like a breeze of sound, brought Dauphin to his knees, trembling and supplicant. He murmured his reply, a sound that abutted the angel's words like a stone against silk. The angel nodded again, and the blackness fell in shreds of inky smoke from him. As it did so, before it rejoined him in oily tendrils, Dauphin could see chinks of light; as daylight seen through cracks in cave walls, fire through the smoky glass of a furnace door. This thing was burning inside, it seemed, and the blackness with which it shrouded itself was protection, Dauphin realised. Without it, the thing would fly apart into its fiery whole, larger than worlds, wiser than civilisations, purer than the very air that sustained it. Dauphin reached a shaking hand towards it, and cried out when it took a step backwards. He touched a hand to a trailing thread of blackness, and it felt like he had lost that limb to eternity. The thread drew back towards its designer, keen to be part of the thing, and Dauphin's hand seemed withered, atrophied without its touch.

"Why?" asked the angel.

Dauphin looked at it. He formed an answer but was shaken by this second question. He had expected the stroke to come quickly, expected the roar of fire to stab between his legs and mark him forever. He would have gladly died for that stroke, had expected to. Now he knelt before his end, and tried to understand what was being asked of him. None of the other creatures had asked him questions before they delivered the stroke, or bite, or stab. They had done his bidding with little regard for the reasons why. It was in their nature of course, but even so, there had been sentience among some of them, and if he had garnered a few questioning looks before they dealt their blows, they had been only looks. Never this question. Never, *why?*

The thing asked again, more insistent this time, and Dauphin felt its breath as a blast of warmth, and felt a dreadful premonition that the angel would unbind itself from the trappings of darkness that swathed its truth, and burn him where he knelt. The angel's breath reached him again, and this time it seemed to calm his nerves. He was able, this time, to formulate an answer.

"It is what I do," he said simply. "I collect scars as others may collect stamps. They are my way of marking the stages of my life. It is simply what I do."

The angel looked at Dauphin. For the first time, Dauphin seemed able to make sense of its expression and saw there, not unconditional beatific joy as he naively presumed he would have done, but rather a complicated mix of scorn, of love and confusion. Its brow was furrowed, and in the valleys of that furrowing, needle points of light had begun to break out.

"Show me," the angel commanded, its voice now low and full of suffering. Tears had begun to leak from its eyes, their course down his cheeks marked by smoking lines of fiery wetness. The oily surface of his face and hands was roiling now, as if under some invisible pressure from within. He looked like a creature in turmoil.

Dauphin undressed as he was, without standing. It was a complicated affair, made more so by the dark of the room and the reek of the angel, strong in Dauphin's sinuses. He had to stop his undressing more than once to pinch his nostrils shut and to wipe the tears streaming from him. Now naked, his clothes a ragged pile beside him, Dauphin appeared small, withered next to this being.

It took in the sight of his skin's scarification, and there was a huge inrush of air, a fiery back draft that set Dauphin's hair blowing and pulled the sweat away from his chest and thighs, leaving him cold. The angel wept great tears at the sight, and repeated its questions of him.

"Why have you done this?" it begged, its voice louder now, beginning to peak at the limit of Dauphin's tolerance. His ears thrummed with it, and he tried to cover them in an effort to stop the noise. His arms were leaden however, and would not bend to his will. They remained stuck to the floor, as if nailed there. Dauphin began to shake his head, tried to warn the angel that he would soon be deaf to its bemoaning.

There was suddenly silence. In it, Dauphin could hear the stuttering hiss of his own breathing and also the crackle of the angel's. It had lifted a foot or so from the floor and hovered above him, its arms held out, palms up, dripping the blackness from it.

This time when he looked, Dauphin could not see the oily substance rejoining the angel's body. Rather it ran away from him, hid in the corners and shadows of the room. The angel, consequently, was becoming brighter, the fire of its innards showing through more and more as its covering fled. Dauphin now had to contend with the brightness. It was becoming unbearable to see, like looking at a blazing furnace, or into the sun. It hurt to look, and he closed his eyes. Even now, however, the heat at brightness attacked his eyelids. They began to crackle, or he imagined that they did, and he began to moan his fear and pain. The angel began to speak again, forever asking questions.

"What have you done to your body? Why have you asked me here? What can I do for you?" The voice rose in volume and pitch, and now Dauphin's ears became pained. He tried to speak, but it was like breathing into a hurricane. No noise left him, or such insubstantial noise that it was swallowed utterly by the growing conflagration.

He spoke in his head now, unable to open his mouth against the waves of heat that were coming off the angel. He could see right through his eyelids, or had had them burned from his face, and the being appeared swathed in fire, not red or yellow or even white, but some *un-colour*, the antithesis of everything he assumed it would be. Writhing knots of heat-haze filigreed its skin, and in those writhings, he glimpsed a body of perfect symmetry, an utter stillness of form. He marvelled at it, even as it undid him. He could feel the deep crackle of skin on fire, could feel the tightening of his limbs and face as they withered in the heat. And still it berated him with questions.

"Why have you done this? Why?"

He attempted to let known his desires, tried to communicate his wish for its touch in that secret place of smoothness. He gave up on words, and in a show of ludicrous pornography he bared his crotch to the thing, showing the place that he had chosen, parting his thigh and scrotum to have that place laid bare to the thing's touch.

"Scar me!" he managed to gasp, and in doing so, lost his tongue to the fire. It sizzled from his mouth and left him dumb. He was content to speak with his mind, and was rewarded with the mutterings of a thousand languages. They pierced him. He bled from ears and mouth and anus and still was content to kneel before the angel and receive its communion. He thrust his skin towards the angel's hands and smiled through corrupted lips as it drew close, all presentiment gone. The things face was a blur of incandescence, and it reached the sticks of its limbs to him. Fire speared from the tips and enveloped Dauphin. The contours of his skin became a playground for the tendrils of fire, and they found every hole and scab and weal and scar, flickering across each with the tenderness of wind.

Dauphin fell back, his skin cracking as he struck the floor, and his legs lolled obscenely, presenting his chosen patch of skin for the things touch. It reached towards him further, and looked into his eyes.

"Look at me, Dauphin," it said. The questions had stopped.

He turned his crisped eyes the thing's way, struggled to blink the smoke and ash from them, but couldn't.

"I cannot touch you," it said. "I would die to do so."

Dauphin was still, all sight and sound suddenly returned to him anew, clear and without corruption. "Plea...." he started, his arms lifting slowly. Painful tears had begun, cutting through the fresh burns across his face.

"I cannot harm," it continued, "even if it is your desire. I cannot."

Even as he watched, Dauphin could see the angel's fire dimming, losing heat and brightness, becoming the distant roiling blaze of a campfire left to smoulder. It blinked out as the blackness rushed from its shadowy confines to cover it once more. The dark shining thing blazed but not with fire now. It moved from Dauphin to resume its place at the table. Dauphin cried out, and at the sound, the noise and warmth of the angel vanished completely. Even as he watched, it became insubstantial, it became shadow, and then it became nothing. It was gone.

Dauphin screamed. He sat, aware that the skin on his naked body was fresh and pink, no longer scarified, no longer his obsession. His scars had been utterly healed, without exception.

His collection was gone.

Harris, crouching behind the locker, drew the Polaroid and clicked a picture. The camera spat the lolling tongue of paper and Harris snatched it away, firing off another, and another. They all showed the same thing.

Dauphin sat amid the mess of his clothes. His head was bowed, and his eyes were bereft of emotion. Thick tear streaks had washed a path through the dark soot that covered his face, but his body shone with the pink freshness of a moderate flagellant.

Harris went to him and gathered his clothes. He draped the jacket about his shoulders. It was Dauphin who spoke first, and his flat voice chilled Harris.

"It's gone, Harris. All gone."

"Not all gone." Harris said this softly, and elaborated not at all.

* * *

After two weeks, Harris removed the Polaroids from his jacket pocket and laid them face down on the table in Dauphin's room of pictures. Dauphin had not set foot in that room since the day on the docks, but Harris knew he would. Dauphin might not own the collection anymore, but he had proof that he once had. That might be enough. And of course there were those new pictures.

Dauphin would look at them one day, and in so doing, would realise that he had lost nothing. The scars were gone, yes, those you could *see*. But to look at Dauphin in those pictures. To see his eyes, devoid of humanity, devoid of emotion. To see the utter loss that he had endured. To have had the angel within touching distance, to have bared soul and skin alike for its touch, and to have been denied it. To see all that on a man's face.

Surely in that, he had all that he ever wanted.

The angel, in denying Dauphin its touch, in denying him its own mark for his collection, had given him the greatest scar he could ever own. It had scarred his heart, his soul, his very core. He hadn't lost those others. He had simply overcome them, incorporated them into himself so that he was the sum, much more than the sum, of their parts.

He was the scar now.

It had cost Dauphin his fortune, this last, and was a fitting end to his obsession.

Harris smiled and turned the pictures face up, ready for Dauphin, for the time when Dauphin was ready for them.

Crawling the Insect Life

by
Opal Edgar

The needles always felt too large when they crushed through the shimmering wings of beetle carcasses. Mervin paused, job only half-done, this was like skewering a cow with a lamppost, it created so much damage to the general structure of the insect there had to be a better way. He had tried glue and had regretted the inability to the see the belly of his beasts. After a second's more thought, he decided there was no other way. The hardest part now was getting the pin to poke through the abdomen of the insect to the other side, without shattering the brittle membrane of the exoskeleton. He tentatively prodded the inside of the shell, looking through his magnifying glasses so as to guess where the needle point lay. If he wanted the coleoptera to show its antennas just right, there was only one spot the needle could come out. The harsh neon lights left the colors of the beetle as unaltered as if it had been daylight. Mervin held his breath as he jabbed. When the phone rang, he reached the darkened skylight in a single jump.

A jagged slash split the centimeter long insect now resting on Mervin's thumb, still impaled by the needle but only loosely so. Copper oozed and stained Mervin's skin. He stared, anger welling in his chest. It felt as if someone had dared poke a gauging finger in his brain while he made love, picking his most private and suppressed thoughts. It was foul, his body felt sickly warm and in a swift movement he ripped the phone line out the wall, dust and chunks of paint flying. White cord wrapped around his hand, he shattered

141

the receiver with the heel of his shoe in a satisfying crunch. A tar monster bubbled up the handset, faceted eyes sliding up and down its slimy body, shimmering like gangrene-filled blow flies. It flew up to buzz about Mervin's head. Only then, with the black horror laughing at the scattered plastic about the room, Mervin noticed his trembling hands. It took a while for the information to ripple up his nerves and sizzle brain cells. The intensity of the anger shocked him out of it and embarrassed he laughed at the absurdity of the situation. This was just a bug, just one tiny little common bug, and he had thousands of them to ruin. The black monster popped into trails of sticky substance and out of existence, leaving Mervin lightheaded as if he'd yawned blocked ears away.

Dropping the beetle into the wastebasket, Mervin got up and stretched his large back. He spent way too many hours parked in his office chair. Once he had run for an hour every morning, forcing another hour of crunches at night, and routinely pushed metal at the gym. But he didn't do any of that anymore, hard muscles had grown soft and started to bulge under tight shirts he'd never thought to replace. He hadn't even noticed the change until one day he'd seen his skin flow over his waistband. At first he'd panicked. Was that aging? But then he'd let it slide, like all the rest for that matter. He didn't remember exactly when he'd started letting things lapse, during the divorce perhaps, or when his father had gotten sick. Because he had to be available at odd times, he'd stopped the weekly mountaineering to hunt the wild insects and bought terrariums so he didn't have to go out anymore. Now his insects bred on their own. He just had to spend a few minutes a week dropping dead wood, flowers, and a little water in. What took time was the taxidermy.

Mervin walked to the door of the office, followed by a large green mass that left a slimy trail over the carpet. He walked right past the glass showcases of beetles and rows of chemicals. The office smelled ephemeral, as if in a moment of absentmindedness, the flick of a match would cause the whole place to explode into flames. No ether fumes remained, but the permanently locked windows and doors had made the smell everlasting. It impregnated the wallpaper and clung to the furniture in ghostly remnants of eternalized insects. The showcases flowed through the corridors, starting from the floor and reaching the ceiling. Mervin had them custom made. He would have liked to carve and sand and lacquer the wood himself, but he was allergic to wood dust. At least that's what he told himself, but then again he didn't have much spare time — filling those cabinets took way too much of it already. Terrariums replaced the showcases in the main part of the house. They were scattered all over, on the kitchen bench, next to the TV, by the window, on the coffee table, in the guest chair... Mervin knew it was a little over the top, but he rarely had guests anyway and the damned insects kept on breeding no matter how fast he worked at the taxidermy.

The green eyeless, mouthless, lifeless slug followed on, leaving parts of itself behind to remind Mervin of how many times he had made this ridiculous journey between his office and the rest of the house.

Tomorrow was Monday. He'd have to sit through another awful business day, waiting for his ex-wife to boss him into smiling on the phone with clients. The slug dripped corrosive pus-colored fluids, which ate at Mervin's rubber soles and the linoleum. Mervin used to walk barefoot in his house before the divorce, now he had to buy a new pair of shoes every week. He knew he should have gotten a new job, but it wasn't easy.

Opening the fridge door, Mervin nudged the pile of boxed Lebanese takeout to the side, hoping a beer was hiding amongst its fellow junk foods, but none was. He probably had a warm bottle somewhere he could have shoved in the freezer, but there was no room for beer. The freezer was too full of boxes waiting for his attention, and if he looked inside, he'd spend another few hours locked in his office. Still, he wondered how it was going in there, almost forgetting the existence of the green blob on his foot.

Could he chance a peek?

The rubber seal of the freezer door cracked as Mervin put his weight on the handle, hesitating between want and self-control. It was like when he was small and everyone lay presents on the side table for his birthday. He was allowed to see them, almost to touch them, but couldn't open them until the last morsel of the cake was gone. One year he'd choked on the crumbly mouthfuls in his haste to get over the ordeal. He'd never dared tell his mum he preferred those normal days when they didn't have desert because it was too expensive. Somehow, he knew she would have been sad to know he didn't like sweets. The freezer door swung open with the slightest pressure. Mervin had forgotten about his dilemma during his existential questioning of parental relationships. A cloud of cold insect souls escaped the frozen drawer. The mist took a few seconds to dissipate in the smoldering summer heat. Tupperware dishes of murdered beetles materialized from the fog. Mervin gingerly lifted a dish up, careful so as not to break any little legs. Frost clouded the plastic, and he had to break the seal to see if this revolutionary killing method was a success.

The beetle lay on its back, huddled in a corner with legs hugged to its abdomen, exactly as Mervin would expect to find his own frozen body in a meat locker. The thought only crossed his mind fleetingly. Disappointment quickly replaced it. If the legs stayed shriveled as they were now when back at room temperature, the whole batch of beetles would be useless. Dejected, Mervin slammed the box on his counter and whacked the drawer back into its arctic cave. The acid of the green slime had done its job better than usual and acrid fumes burned Mervin's eyes. This thing was going to give him cancer, just like his dad's. He simply knew it. He coughed as he grabbed the slug between thumb and index finger. Was it his imagination, or had the thing grown again? It felt like it was at least eight kilograms now.... Soon he'd have to go to the doctor to get it weighed. How long had he been putting off the appointment?

He dropped the slug in the sink and mopped the floor. The laces of his shoes smoldered to dust. He'd have to wear his shoes as loafers for the rest of the evening. Soles trailing, he reached the sofa, but before he sat down, he noticed the terrarium in the guest chair filling with black. He blinked as a dollop fell in from the heavens. Tar covered the ceiling. Reflective eyes, forever moving and sliding into the soft fleshy substance, dripped down to become rising goop in the terrarium. Mervin swore and snatched the glass case from the chair. A hundred little beetles floated on their backs trapped in the bog. Putting the terrarium in the chair had been a bad idea. But oppressive loneliness had squeezed his chest with prickly purple tentacles. He couldn't help it, he'd dropped the insects in the guest chair. They were the only companions he had left. And now they were dead, and he couldn't even immortalize them the way he so much desired, like good memories happily trapped forever in his mind. Tar dripped on his hand and circled his wrist like a cold forgotten wedding band. The blank slug was back, trailing after him.

They were growing in number; Mervin couldn't help but notice, as if they were trying to fill the hollowness. Scrubbing at the glass and throwing clumps of dirt and wood into the sink, he wondered how long this could go on. He wasn't exactly the friendliest fellow, but the specters were feeding the growing social vacuum around him. He told himself he didn't care, but then he remembered those happy years when he'd partied with any occasional friend that came his way. The wet grit embedded under his fingernails made heavy *ploc* noises at it came down onto the metal. When had he started changing like that? The tar leaked down and clogged the drain but wouldn't come off the glass surfaces of the terrarium, no matter how much Mervin rubbed. It took 20 manic minutes of useless effort for Mervin to give up. He threw an appalled look at his green featureless slug and carried the aquarium to the curb — perhaps it was only ruined to him.

Stepping into the entrance hall, Mervin paused and for once looked around himself at the dead insects. Each little beetle on the wall was an exact copy of the one next to it. It could have been wallpaper. Mervin had chosen all of them to be the same exact shape, color and size. They were all catalogued and pinned down by the same loving hand. Mervin read this as the confirmation of his insanity, and under his self-loathing gaze, the green slime took on another five hundred grams. It had never grown so quickly in one shot before. His wife had been embarrassed when he had worked on a small-scaled insect collection, as if this was a hobby only Norman Bates could indulge. What would she say if she saw it now? Not that she came to the house anymore. She found him repulsive, he could see it in the crisp lines around her mouth, and in the coldness of her eyes when she looked at him. When they first met, she'd found his habit of bug collecting cute, a confirmation of a softer side to his muscle mass. She didn't understand that this was the only gift his father had given him.

The cold husk of a man in the funeral home couldn't have been Mervin's dad. That thing in a suit was a masquerading stick insect. Eventually, Mervin accepted the death, and it came as a bruising hit. He would never see his father again, and he would never know if the man had ever loved him.

The tar shone on the ceiling and dribbled down the walls. Mervin was tired. Would his dad have loved him if he'd become an entomologist like him? Would he have accepted him if he'd been smarter? Mervin had taken too long to understand that he could have gotten friends without being a semi-pro footballer, and that admiration wasn't friendship. It faded overnight. Mervin didn't bother to get the slug off his foot as he walked to the back of the house.

The bathroom light blinked a few times before coming on. Mervin's eyes looked back at him underlined by dark circles. They had appeared one day in the mirror, after another sleepless night. When he'd noticed them, he grew scared. Mervin had never seen a trace of his father in himself before, apart from his odd shade of grey blond hair, but at that instant, he saw that his dad had taken his eyes over and spread his vision onto Mervin's world. Mervin's father had been a busy man, working instead of living. When Mervin's mother had found another man to notice her, Mervin's father had been left with a little boy with a foreign ritual of eating habits and talking patterns. Mervin had been seven. He was scared when he came back from school to the empty creaking house that reminded him monsters waited around every corner to skin him like the ox tongues his mother use to prepare.

The toothpaste froth swirled down the drain. Mervin examined his teeth. He'd had to throw the slug off his leg twice in as many minutes because it kept climbing over him. Goosebumps covered his legs, and millions of beetles, like so many soldiers leading a prisoner to execution, supervised the dreaded walk to the bed. This was his hell. Between the empty sheets, Mervin couldn't hide the absence of a caring presence in his life anymore. Every night, in his large double bed, he stared at the emptiness.

Forehead pressed to the door of the bedroom, Mervin had to gather strength before the ritual could proceed. His wife must have known how much he'd suffer when she left him the custom-made bed.

After fifteen minutes of dread, Mervin pushed the bedroom door open. It was work in itself considering all the creatures agglomerated in there, bubbling from the ceiling and walls and cupboards and floor. They reached his waist now and rolled over each other, inside each other, popping in and out of existence, merging and swimming over his flat pillow-less bed. No, the soft, slimy creatures hadn't eaten the bedding; Mervin had simply gotten rid of the pillows. He was a simple man of simple tastes, and pillows left him feeling awkward and sleepless when they engulfed his head in their soft folds. Pillows felt, he wasn't quite sure what, but if he'd thought about it, he might have said suffocating.

Undressing amongst the slime was awkward. His

clothes disappeared inside the goo. Usually, in the morning, the monsters disappeared long enough for him to find them again.

The bed was comfortable and so damned big and pink. His wife had chosen the fabric. She sewed it into quilt covers and pillowcases during her student phase of 'back to the origins.' The fabric was the exact shade of pink as the flowers growing on the Azalea bush in the back garden. She'd loved those flowers, and the day she'd left him that was all she'd taken. He'd come back from the hospital and found her in the back garden with a spade, digging up the surprisingly extensive root system. She'd yelled at him even before he'd asked what was going on. She couldn't take him anymore, she'd said, shaking the uprooted bush in her hand as testament. Dirt and tiny centimeter long cerambycidae beetles had flown out. He'd caught one as she'd dumped the flowers on the car seat and drove off with grit-covered hands.

With his proud antennas propped up by a well-placed pin, that very beetle accusingly pointed at him from behind a little glass case hanging close to the bed. Its clones covered the rest of the house.

The sheets felt wet as Mervin slid into them. Once, he had asked himself if you could die of yearning. The answer was yes. As the specters of dead hope grew and multiplied in Mervin's sleepless night, they rolled over his face, attracted like chicklings to their mother. At first, Mervin lazily swatted at them like they were flies. They weren't just trying to lay by him, close to him; they were reaching into his nostrils, plugging his ears and crawling into his mouth. He tried to grab them, but they slid wherever they wanted, squeezed however they desired. They filled his mouth, slipping through his fingers like water. They slid down his throat to touch him on the heart and remind him that it still beat. It was too late. Aborted dreams had lost their meaning to him, and they only choked him further. Mervin had gotten his answer, as he lay cold — finally free of his cumbersome emotions.

The Room Beneath the Stairs

by
Kealan Patrick Burke

Andy hated being forced to visit his grandmother.

As he watched his parents drive away in their battered Taurus, he once again found himself beneath the ivy-choked architrave that led into her terribly small and tangled garden. It made him wish his brother was still alive to do it but this in turn made him feel guilty. Before Steven had died, the task of representing parents who really couldn't be bothered to visit the old woman had been his charge.

Andy had only been to Gramma West's house a handful of times but it had been enough.

Even with his family around, he had felt threatened by something lurking in the permanent shadows of the old lady's home but those unseen watchers seemed patient to wait until he came by himself.

And now he was.

He quickly made his way up the narrow bramble-bordered path and wished he were somewhere else. Intimidating houses were not the place for a twelve-year-old boy on sunny Saturday mornings. He'd much rather be playing with Jimmy, the boy next door, or watching *Transformers* on the Cartoon Network.

Dewdrops glistened and dangled from black thorns like poison from the fangs of serpents. His discomfort seemed to draw the stares of invisible things. He felt a thousand hungry eyes on him, aroused by the scent of adolescent panic, hiding behind blankets of ivy and watching, waiting.

Lifting the bronze knocker he thumped three times and waited a short forever before the door whooshed open and a florid rosy-cheeked face peered around the opening.

"Hey, Gramma."

The old lady swung into full view and made a face that suggested she might cry.

"Andy! Oh, how good of you to come see your Gramma!"

Her considerable frame heaved forward and swallowed Andy in an embrace tight enough to make him gasp. Just as he was beginning to formulate a polite protest, she released him and gestured for him to enter the house.

"Come, come!"

Beaming at him, she vanished inside with an agility that belied her eighty-three years.

Andy took a deep breath and stepped over the threshold into the gloomy hallway.

He followed his grandmother into the kitchen but not before casting a wary eye at the heavy oak door beneath the stairs. A thin shard of hazy amber light seeped through a crack in the wood as if someone was shining a torch through from the other side.

He recalled the last time he'd been here; the scraping noise that had come from inside the room. Despite his fear, he had approached the door with the intention of flinging it wide to gaze upon the horror it undoubtedly contained, but had scarcely touched the knob when Gramma West appeared behind him. He had almost suffered a heart attack when her pale hand fell on his shoulder.

"Hey, Gramma?" he asked as he entered the kitchen, pleasantly surprised by the thick aroma of freshly baked apple pies that greeted him.

"Yes, dear?"

"What's behind that door beneath the stairs?"

He half-expected her to tense and turn to look at him, the still piping hot pie slipping from her oven mitt, a guilty look on her bespectacled face.

"Oh, the devil is locked behind that door, Andy. He keeps

me fit and healthy and I feed him little boys who are foolish enough to ask questions," she didn't say.

Instead, she raised her eyebrows and offered him a cheerful smile that made her cheeks puff up to twice their normal size.

"Oh, that was your grandfather's workroom. He was always a bit upset that we had no back garden or cellar for him to build a tool shed, so he used the room beneath the stairs. It's plenty big. Surprisingly so."

She opened the oven door and as Andy took a seat at the large pine table in the center of the room, he asked: "Can I see it?"

She wheezed as she bent over to slide two more pies into the oven.

"There's nothing to see in there, Andy. Just junk. I haven't given it the cleaning I've been promising myself I would. Can't bear to face it to be honest. Too many memories of your grandfather."

She took a seat opposite Andy, who was now picturing trans-dimensional portals hidden beneath stairwells.

"Some day when I get around to fixing it up, you can investigate to your heart's content."

Andy nodded. Her attempt at appeasing his curiosity had only further inflamed it, however, and he resolved to make another attempt to peek inside the room before he left.

"So how are things at home?" Gramma asked, poking the bridge of her glasses back into place.

He told her everything his parents had told him to tell her. Mostly lies. His home life since Steven's death had rapidly decayed and now their once benign unit had become a somber vigil to a stolen child. His parents went about their daily routine like hollow vessels, acting only on memories gleaned from happier times.

His grandmother's eyes told him she knew most of what he said had been from a script approved by his parents and that it was okay.

"I expect they'll end up spoiling you yet, Andy. Parents

who've lost a child tend to lavish affection on the remaining one once the initial impact of grief subsides."

Andy nodded and drummed his fingers on the table. He was already bored and uncomfortable talking about his life with a woman practically a stranger to him.

"I suppose," he replied.

She clapped her hands together. "So how 'bout some pie?"

"Sure."

As they ate, Andy noticed the old woman staring at him with an intensity that made him squirm. He tried to reason she was simply glad to see him, but couldn't bring himself to believe it.

"You look a lot like your grandfather, you know," she said at last, breaking the silence forming like a pane of ice between them.

Andy raised his eyebrows in response, his mouth full of baked apples. He had been stuffing himself almost greedily as an excuse not to talk to her.

She looked at him with dark green eyes filled with remembrance.

"When he was young, I mean. Same chin, same ears. You even eat the same way as Ben."

Andy blushed, juice leaking from the corner of his mouth.

"You have the same hands too — a craftsman's hands. Elegant in a rough sort of way."

The boy dropped his gaze to his long, thin fingers. He quite liked her description of them. He had always just thought of them as...well, as hands. Now they were something much more. Now he had *craftsman's* hands. He smiled.

"There was nothing your grandfather couldn't make with his hands. When we were younger and moved into that terrible rattrap on Haybury Street, he made it into a little palace. The landlord refused to charge us rent for the next few months after he saw what Ben had done with the place. I imagine he was quite pleased when he thought of how much he could charge for it after we moved out."

Her eyes glazed over and Andy continued to eat, aware she wasn't actually looking at him anymore but using him as a focal point for her trip down memory lane.

"He built cabinets, tables, and chairs. Anything we needed and couldn't afford, he went out and chopped down a few trees from his father's place and made himself. By the time he was finished, the house looked nothing like it had when we first moved in."

She smiled, revealing polished dentures, and put her hand atop Andy's. The boy resisted the urge to pull away and secretly chided himself for being so cruel. Although he didn't know her and her house made him uneasy, she was still his grandmother. Plus, the pie was terrific.

"Another thing about Ben was that he was a pleasant character and made friends easily, whereas I was perfectly happy to stay at home, cooking and cleaning. I doubt there are very many women left these days who'd be so content with that!"

She chuckled and Andy grinned awkwardly, the humor lost on him.

"He began to do work for his friends, a favor here, a favor there, until word began to spread about the quality of his work. Soon the jobs were pouring in and so was the money. We went from being a struggling couple, held together by love and not much else, to a relatively well-to-do couple that could afford things we'd only dreamed about in the past.

"We moved out of Haybury and into this fine house, with plenty of money left over to think about starting a family. And so, we did. The day your father was born changed everything for us."

She stroked Andy's hand with her forefinger, a rueful smile on her face. The boy found his interest piqued despite himself and he abandoned his study of the cobwebs in the far corner of the room.

"We knew raising a child would not be easy and as Ben was up to his neck in work he'd been contracted to do, I was left with the task of bringing up your father. However, there were times when my husband would find himself summoned from his much needed slumber to deal with the wails of a hungry baby. Even when the child was distressed and filled the house with screams, Ben's hands would soothe it back to sleep. There was nothing he couldn't do. More pie?"

Andy was confused for a second by the change of subject and, when he realized what she was asking, shook his head and thanked her.

She nodded and continued to stroke his hand. Her skin was soft and supple on his.

"This went on for a year or so. If I was so tired that I wouldn't wake immediately, Ben would go to the baby and feed him, change his diaper, or stroke him back to sleep. I should have known at the time that he would not be able to continue like that without it having some kind of adverse effect on him."

"Adverse?" Andy interrupted, now so engrossed in the tale he didn't want any of it to pass him by.

"Bad. I knew it would end in disaster. We never argued. Well, not enough to worry about anyway. So when he began to grow irritable, I put it down to the long workdays and the inconvenience of having to tend to the baby whenever I deserted my post."

She took her hand away and clasped them together beneath her chin.

The sunlight that filtered in through the kitchen window to Andy's left made her eyes glisten and he found himself hoping she wouldn't weep. Such an outburst of emotion from his grandmother would leave him embarrassed and helpless.

"But it eventually came to a point where I was beginning to question whether or not he loved me anymore. His bouts of irritation turned to anger too fast for me not to be concerned. His hours grew longer and longer until seeing him home at all became a rare treat. He told me he'd been given a lot of work at the Fallon Mansion where that weird old guy Howie Phillips lived. For much of the time, your father kept me distracted, but lying alone in bed at night I had plenty of time to worry.

"When I confronted him about his hours, he would fly into a rage as if he thought I was accusing him of something. The arguments would end with my questions unanswered and my heart more wounded than ever. As for Ben, he would storm off and lock himself into the room beneath the stairs, where he would continue to work long into the night. As you can imagine, the clamor of his labors upset the child and I would be left dealing with a cranky baby the next day. I grew miserable and lonely."

When Andy spoke, his voice was tiny. "What did you do?"

Her eyes seemed to brighten at his obvious interest and she grinned slightly. "The only thing I could. I walked in on him in the room beneath the stairs and locked the door behind me, blocking any attempt he might have made to escape me."

Andy's eyes widened. A needle of fear pricked the back of his neck. "You didn't..."

Gramma West looked shocked. "Oh Dear Lord, no! I would never have done anything to hurt him. You must understand, Andy, that despite the fact he seemed to have lost all love for me, I still cared for him as much as always. The thought of losing him was unbearable and because he wouldn't speak to me, I imagined all sorts of unpleasant things he might be doing while not in my company.

"That night, he was outraged at my invasion of his sanctuary and tried to throw me out. I stood my ground, more out of shock than defiance. I could hardly believe what my eyes were showing me. But when he noticed that I had seen the fruit of his labors, he seemed to slump, and for the first time in months he spoke to me like the Ben I remembered, the man I loved."

Andy found himself leaning forward slightly, eager to hear what his grandfather had hidden in the room he, himself, was so curious to see.

"He had been in the middle of carving something. A figurine. From what I could see of it, it looked to be a rendition of a woman. It would go perfectly well with the thousands of others piled around him. Some of them were scattered about his feet, others stacked against the walls so high they squeezed beneath the slope of the stairs. All of them were carved from a light wood, maple perhaps, but not all of them were the same.

"As I scanned them in disbelief that he should be forsaking his family for such a repetitive hobby, I noticed that, amid the stacks of wooden men and children, there were monsters. Here was a representation of a woman with her hands to her face, screaming. There, an ill-formed, man-shaped thing with lovingly carved tentacles sprouting from its chest.

"Some were cowering wolf-like creatures with mouths full of jagged teeth and wild eyes. Others were so vile it hurt my eyes to look at them. And in the center of them all with a work-in-progress clutched tightly in his fist, stood my husband.

"He told me I should have stayed away from things that were none of my concern. This made me laugh out loud, Andy, it really did. I told him he was my concern and that I had only come to his little room to find out what was keeping him from his family, what was so important to him that he preferred their company to ours."

She sighed and fingered a curl of silver hair, her eyes boring through the kitchen table and Andy found himself wondering if his grandfather had made it.

"He had fallen in love with his own ability to create. And still, I tried to rationalize what I was seeing. Perhaps he had fallen into debt and been forced or consigned to produce thousands of odd little figurines in return. Perhaps it was just a large order he had received from someone, someone like Phillips. I thought these things and tried to tell myself that it had to be something that innocent. Only the look of shame and fear in my husband's eyes convinced me otherwise. That, and the sinking feeling in my bosom that whatever had taken hold of Ben wouldn't ever let him go.

"Eventually he told me everything."

She let her eyes drift around the room, settling on the window as she spoke.

"He told me it was his hands. He told me that the very things he relied upon to keep his family content were now responsible for trying to take them away. I didn't understand and I told him so. He sat down and hung his head, looking defeated and exhausted, and I went to him. When he flinched at my touch, I almost cried, deciding in that instant that I would fight his demons for him if it came to a point where he was unable to do so himself.

"His love for his work had died almost without him noticing, but he had snapped to attention one night in the middle of carving one of the figurines and realized that he had been in a daze, a trance of some sort and had made almost three-hundred of the ghastly things in an hour. He was up to his ankles in wood shavings with no recollection of ever carving them. He said that some of the statues were imitations of the child and me. Others, he didn't know quite what they were, but they were all things he had seen in dreams...or nightmares.

"He was being driven by some unwanted compulsion, what he called 'an outside influence,' to carve these things, and it scared him half to death whenever he came back to himself and found he had made a hundred more. Would it continue to make him work until they filled the house, the streets, the town?

"He had no answers for his own questions and I could not answer for him. I was just as scared by his revelations but not for the same reasons.

"I was beginning to doubt his sanity, you see. I thought

that perhaps he had overworked himself into a fever and the threads of his composure were beginning to unravel. I felt guilty not believing him, but who would?

"His story continued in the same vein. He was not in control of his hands. A higher power was using him as a tool to make these ugly wooden statues. He did not know why but suspected its motives were not entirely wholesome. He begged me for help and as I held him in my arms in that small little room beneath the stairs where my husband carved out his madness, I promised I would help him."

She looked back to Andy, who was hanging on her every word. He had already made up his mind that if his grandmother had a vault of such stories he would be back again to hear them. These tales, undoubtedly embellished but no less powerful because of it, were like some of the stories he read in his brother's *Weird Tales* magazines. Gramma West's stories were a lot scarier though, simply because their roots were buried in truth somewhere. Half the appeal for Andy was not knowing how much was real and how much was made up.

"I took him from the room, his workshop, and brought him upstairs to bed, where he slept fitfully for a few hours and awoke weeping. I sat vigil by his side watching the sleeping pills take effect and his hands carve figurines above his chest. My own tears were silent as I watched whatever sickness held him in its grasp using him like a puppet. At times he would wake screaming, howling unintelligible phrases at the ceiling. As he slept, his hands would carve, and sometimes his nails would peel the skin from his hands until I gently pried them apart and set them on his stomach.

"I watched him die, Andy. I watched the terror his mind inflicted on him act itself out in one final display of shrieked gibberish and wide-eyed panic until his heart gave out and he collapsed back onto the bed leaving his final breath hovering in the air above him."

She leaned closer to Andy and he swallowed.

"But that's not the worst of it, Andy. Not by a long shot. The worst of it was that, as I watched over his body that night, as I prayed and wept aloud at last, as I rocked myself back and forth and listened to the baby cry in the next room, I was fascinated. Fascinated by his hands, that they could continue to carve their images from the air even as he lay dead beneath them."

"Whoa," Andy breathed. "Is that why you didn't want to show me the room? Because you kept the figurines, right?"

The old woman fixed him with a look of intense sadness and slowly shook her head.

The figurines...

As he looked at her, his eyes widened in horror. He remembered the faint scraping sound from inside the room, the feeling of being watched in the garden. *A thousand hungry eyes.*

Gramma sighed. "I'm afraid I kept a little more than that, Andy."

About the Authors

Jeremy C. Shipp

Jeremy C. Shipp is the Bram Stoker Award-nominated author of Cursed, Vacation, and Sheep and Wolves. His shorter tales have appeared or are forthcoming in over 60 publications, the likes of *Cemetery Dance, ChiZine, Apex Magazine, Withersin,* and *Shroud Magazine.* Jeremy enjoys living in Southern California in a moderately haunted Victorian farmhouse called Rose Cottage. He lives there with his wife, Lisa, a couple of pygmy tigers, and a legion of yard gnomes. The gnomes like him. The clowns living in his attic – not so much. His online home is www.jeremycshipp.com and his twitter handle is @ JeremyCShipp.

Mary Borsellino

Mary writes fiction, pop-culture analysis, comics and music journalism, and whatever else comes out of her head. She also reads like it's going out of style, makes jewellery, goes to as many rock shows as she can, watches a lot of horror movies, says tasteless things in public situations, and finds every excuse she can to travel.

She can usually be found in Melbourne, Australia, where she works as Editor of the journal *Australian Philanthropy.*

Brent Michael Kelley

Brent Michael Kelley lives and writes in the Wisconsin Northwoods. He shares a home with such things as hairless dogs, a snake named Darth Batman, and the woman he married on Halloween. In addition to writing about his pal Chuggie, he likes writing story-poems, painting monsters, and making wine. Some say late at night, if you're alone by a campfire, you can summon Brent by closing your eyes and saying his name eleven times. He insists this is not true and there's no way it will work... yet.

Phil Hickes

Phil recently moved to Wellington, New Zealand, after spells in London, Bristol, Cardiff (UK) and Dublin. During the day he writes for a living in the advertising industry, and at night, he writes his own stuff. Usually something horror-related. He can be found on Twitter @hickesy

L.S. Murphy

LS Murphy lives the Greater St. Louis area where she watches Cardinals baseball, reads every book she can find, and weaves tales for young adults and adults. She can be found at LSMurphy.com and followed on Twitter @LSMurphy

Michael Colangelo

Michael R. Colangelo is a writer from Toronto.

Neil Davies

Neil Davies was born in 1959 and has found everything else to be an uphill struggle. He currently lives in the North West of England with his wife and two children. Any spare time he can find he spends writing. For more information please visit his official website — www.nwdavies.co.uk

Louise Bohmer

Louise Bohmer is a freelance editor and writer based in Sussex, New Brunswick, where, along with rats and a furry husband, she resides under a rock. She edits for Permuted Press, and is an associate editor for KHP Books. Her debut novel The Black Act was released by Library of Horror in 2009, but is now out of print. You can read her short fiction in Old School, The Red Penny Papers, and Courting Morpheus. Her poetry can be read in Death In Common.

Edmund Colell

Edmund Colell is an intern for Eraserhead Press' Lazy Fascist imprint, as well as a college writing tutor, who enjoys collecting gooey pieces of strange medical fiction and facts. His work has appeared in or will be appearing in *Verbicide, LegumeMan, New Flesh, Christmas on Crack, Bizarro Central*, and *Amazing Stories of the Flying Spaghetti Monster.*

S.P. Miskowski

S.P. Miskowski's stories have been published *by Identity Theory, Horror Bound Online Magazine, The Absent Willow Review, Other Voices, The Stranger* and *New Times*, and will appear in *Supernatural Tales 21*. She received two Swarthout prizes for fiction as an undergraduate, and two National Endowment for the Arts fellowships, one for short stories and one for drama. Her play "my new friends (are so much better than you)" was nominated for the American Theatre Critics Association/Steinberg New Play Award. Her latest play "Emerald City" will be produced by Live Girls! Theater in Spring 2012. She is a member of Wily Writers.

Michael Montoure

An unreliable narrator, Michael Montoure is an indie writer of horror and dark urban fantasy. His obsessions include hidden truths, secret dealings, and the changing and fragile nature of our own pasts. He lives alone with a gray cat by the edge of Echo Lake, Washington, and can be found online at www.bloodletters.com. He is standing right behind you.

Lee Widener

In the past, Lee Widener has written mainly for the theatre. His one act play "Emergency Parking Only" received a staged reading at the Stark Raving Theater in Portland, Oregon. He has had recent publications in online zines *Yesteryear Fiction* and *Farther Stars*, and the print zine *Paper Radio*. For the past eleven years he has operated the internet radio station Never Ending Wonder Radio. www.NeverEndingWonder.com. He is also creator of the Welcome to Weirdsville Cartoon Art series. www.WelcomeToWeirdsville.com

Pete Clark

Pete Clark has a number of short stories published on webzines, and 5 upcoming print publications for 2011 / 2012. He was recently awarded an Honourable Mention in the L. Ron Hubbard Writers of the Future contest. He includes Stephen King, Clive Barker and China Miéville among his many influences. Currently writing numerous short stories and the outline of a novel, he lives in North West England with his wife, two children and a growing collection of guitars.

Opal Edgar

Opal Edgar was born in Australia, and grew up in France. Following in the footsteps of her hero, Kurt Vonnegut, she studied anthropology. Today she spends most of her time cramping many words on tiny bits of flying paper she then has trouble deciphering; so instead she reads Robin McKinley and Jane Austen. She has previously been published by *Aurora Wolf*, *Hungur Magazine* and has upcoming stories in the *Dance Macabre* anthology by Edge, and the *Behind Locked Doors* anthology by Wicked East Press. You can find her writing lone messages on her blog: darkdemonproductions. blogspot.com. Don't hesitate to drop by.

Kealan Patrick Burke

Kealan Patrick Burke is the Bram Stoker Award-winning author of over a dozen books, among them, *The Turtle Boy*, *The Hides*, *Vessels*, *Currency of the Souls*, *Master of the Moors*, and *Kin*. You can find him on the web at www. kealanpatrickburke.com, or via his blog at kealanpatrick. wordpress.com.

About the Editors

Kate Jonez

Kate Jonez writes dark fantasy fiction. Her novel Candy House is under submission and might just see publication in 2012. She is also chief editor at Omnium Gatherum omniumgatherumedia.com, a small press specializing in dark fantasy and transgressive fiction. When she's not writing, editing, or doing publishing chores, she reads, takes photos, investigates odd and obscure historical stuff, and collects things in jars. Visit her personal website at katejonez.com.

S.S. Michaels

S. S. Michaels is a writer of transgressive fiction. She holds degrees in Business Administration and Film & Video Production. She has lived abroad, traveled widely, jumped out of an airplane, and driven a racecar. In film and television, she read slush and wrote coverage, then moved on to become a production coordinator. She finally served as a TV network financial analyst before leaving Hollywood. She lives with her husband, two kids, and two dogs. Visit her blog at slushpilehero.wordpress.com. Her debut novel, Idols & Cons, is getting excellent reviews and is available on Amazon.